From the reviews of the French-language version of
Exile in the Kingdom—

"The term 'masterpiece' is certainly bandied about and misused, but there are certain works that merit the name more than others. *Exile in the Kingdom* is just such a work, both because of its masterful writing, and because of the way Robert Harnum stops short of inflicting upon us the usual message: 'Wake up! Something is happening to our children!'"
—Bertrand Puard, *Magazine Hachette Littérature*

"A novelist who frightens America . . . exactly what about this book so scares America? No doubt it's that Harnum, with a calculating and cold lucidity, places his finger directly in the present day American wound: violence . . . And Philip Andrew Carmichael, the only voice in this novel, is really nothing more, after all, than an ordinary boy."
—*Livres Hebdo*

"Here is a novel that is everything, everything, that is, but a work full of sordid and bloody scenes . . . Robert Harnum gambles by undertaking the incredibly difficult and dangerous task of putting himself, and us, under the skin of one of these kids who suddenly, one day, and for whatever reason, loses control."
—Christophe Rodriguez, *Ici*, Montreal

"Without ever being so pretentious as to try and explain, without ever donning the robe of a moralist, Robert Harnum puts us in Philip's shoes and we live his tragedy, step by step. Even better than that, we become one with this boy-killer who reminds us of adolescents that we all know—that we were once ourselves—in whom the slightest spark can set off the explosion."

—Tristan Malavoy-Racine, *Voir*

"Curiously enough, and more than any other element, it's the indifference, the emotional sterility of the young man that gives so much power to this novel. At no time does Philip Carmichael reflect on the destruction, at no time does he seek an explanation . . . And so, for the love of God, how have we, as a society, arrived at this point? With great narrative mastery, by craftily playing with the unstated, Robert Harnum succeeds in depicting the violent 'malaise' of an individual, of a generation, and in truth, of an entire era. Disturbing? You bet!"   —*Journal de Montréal*

"Robert Harnum puts the reader in a very uncomfortable position. How can we condemn a good and normal boy? And how can we pardon him when he himself finds no reason to do so? . . . Harnum shows how we have surrounded ourselves with structures that blind us from the essential in life."

—Magalie Goumaz, *Magazine Avant-Der*, Switzerland

"'This is not a documentary,' [Harnum] says. 'The truth is in the sensual and artistic experience of the novel. You (the reader) are wearing Philip's skin.' And to be in Philip's skin means coming face to face with the responsibility of each individual towards his or her actions."   —Rémy Charest, *Le Soleil*

exile in the kingdom

OTHER BOOKS BY ROBERT HARNUM

Le festin des lions
Poursuite

exile
in the kingdom

robert harnum >>>

UNIVERSITY PRESS OF NEW ENGLAND *Hanover & London*

Published by
University Press of New England,
Hanover, NH 03755
© 2001 by Robert Harnum
All rights reserved
Printed in the United States of America
5 4 3 2 1

Library of Congress
Cataloging-in-Publication Data
Harnum, Robert.
   Exile in the kingdom / Robert Harnum.
      p. cm. — (Hardscrabble books)
    ISBN 1–58465–148–2 (cloth : alk. paper)
    1. Alienation (Social psychology)—Fiction.
2. Violence in adolescence—Fiction. 3. High school
students—Fiction. 4. Trials (Murder)—Fiction.
5. Police murders—Fiction. 6. Assault rifles—Fiction.
7. Teenage boys—Fiction. 8. Maine—Fiction.
I. Title. II. Series.
PS3608.A75 E93 2001
813'.6—dc21   2001001366

Originally published in French as
La dernière sentinelle by Èditions du
Masque, Paris, in 1999.

HARDSCRABBLE BOOKS
— Fiction of New England

G. F. Michelsen, *Hard Bottom*

Anne Whitney Pierce, *Rain Line*

Kit Reed, *J. Eden*

Rowland E. Robinson (David Budbill, ed.),
   Danvis Tales: Selected Stories

Roxana Robinson, *Summer Light*

Rebecca Rule, *The Best Revenge: Short Stories*

R. D. Skillings, *How Many Die*

R. D. Skillings, *Where the Time Goes*

Lynn Stegner, *Pipers at the Gates of Dawn: A Triptych*

Theodore Weesner, *Novemberfest*

W. D. Wetherell, *The Wisest Man in America*

Edith Wharton (Barbara A. White, ed.),
   Wharton's New England: Seven Stories and Ethan Frome

Thomas Williams, *The Hair of Harold Roux*

To Anne McLennan . . .

for her propelling faith and lasting presence.

And especially, of course, to my mother,
Alda Eslin Harnum.

part one

friday > > >

Yesterday, my stepfather died. Or at least I call him my stepfather, but he was really my mother's boyfriend. My real stepfather is the guy I grew up with.

He had a heart attack, I guess. And that's weird, him dying of a heart attack. I mean he always kept himself in such good shape. Everyday he got up early and went to a gym. And just last year he had a Universal put in downstairs that cost him 12,000 dollars. He was always on that thing. This chart came with it, and it's down there now spread across an entire wall. It shows how to exercise every single muscle group in the human body. He's also got a jogging machine down there. It registers your heart rate, your blood pressure, your breathing rate. As you jog, it breaks everything down into digital units that flash back what it calls "the optimal amount of stress." That cost him about 4,000, or I think that's what he told me. Before he got the Universal, he was on that jogging machine all the time. And he always ate good, too, real good. He watched everything. He made these milkshakes in the blender, with powder from bottles with abbreviations on them, DHEA and GLE, names like that. There's two big boxes full in the kitchen. A couple times a week he'd stop me and say, "I look pretty good for fifty, don't I? What do you think? Not bad, huh kid?" When I didn't answer, he'd just wave me off like he always did, and call me an unresponsive jerk. Yesterday, though, he had a heart attack I guess, in his office, massive. He was a psychologist.

This morning when I woke up it was snowing. I remembered I had a game tonight. A big game. I wasn't nervous, but I never get nervous until about three hours before. Sometimes I even forget. I like that, when I forget, because it all comes pouring back in a couple of hours before, real concentrated. But some of the guys are nervous for days. In seventh period yesterday, Jimmy and Nate already had butterflies. To me, it serves no purpose.

As I said, when I woke up this morning it was snowing. Down in the kitchen, my mother had my suit pressed, hanging in the doorway. She even had breakfast ready. I can't remember the last time she had a breakfast ready. I usually get myself some cereal, or put a couple of strawberry Pop-Tarts in the microwave, I like Pop-Tarts, but my mother had French toast there with cinnamon on the top. She seemed upset, too. She was quiet. My mother's always complaining about something. She never stops, about work, or life, or age. But this morning she was quiet, upset. And I was surprised. I mean, she couldn't stand the guy. They hardly talked anymore. They didn't even sleep in the same fucking room. He moved in when I was in seventh grade. When he did, I guess he made her sign some kind of a legal agreement. After five years together, if they ever broke up, she'd get twenty thousand dollars for every year after those five. According to my mother, that's why he still lived here. Or at least that's why we didn't leave. Neither of 'em could afford to get rid of the other. But for the last couple of years my mother couldn't stand him. She tells me everything, even when I don't want to hear it, and she was always bitching about how if it wasn't for the money, she'd have left the asshole long ago.

Like I said, when I woke up it was snowing. I'd never been to a wake before, either. I had to stand beside my mother. Flowers were everywhere. Delivery men kept bringing them in. They made a path down into this room where my mother's boyfriend, Sidney, laid in a coffin. And lots of old people were there. I had to shake everyone's hand. They all signed this book, and then little old ladies passed by with these cold little scrunched up hands, fish hands. They all smiled and told my mother what a handsome young man I was. It was pretty strange.

I went into the room with the coffin. My mother's boyfriend had his hands crossed over in front. The hairs looked like they were swirling up out of wax. His skin was real pale, blue almost. People stood by the coffin. They talked and looked down at him, nodding their heads. Then his mother and father came in from New York. They didn't even speak to my mother. But I guess they've never spoken to my mother.

Around eleven o'clock, my friend Jason came in dressed in a suit. We went into the bathroom together and he stood on the toilet seat, put his mouth up close to the ventilator, and smoked a joint. He asked me if I wanted some, but I said no because of the game tonight. He kept after me, though, so I finally climbed up on the toilet seat and took a couple of small hits. I don't know what it was, the time of day, the type of dope, or just what, but I really felt it. Then Jason started imitating everyone outside and we both started to laugh. I don't know how long it was before we were able to leave the bathroom, but when we did my mother was pretty upset.

And being stoned at a wake; it's not something I'd recommend, I don't think.

Just before noon I went to school. It was still snowing. The wind was blowing hard, right at me, and the snow caught in my collar, stung my face. But I didn't mind. It felt good actually. I couldn't figure out why until I realized I was stoned. I panicked

a little. I mean I'd never been to school stoned before. Some of
my friends have, lots of times, but they always fool around and
get kicked out of class, or spend half the day in the bathroom.
I don't. And when I smoke dope things squeeze in. If I'm in the
right place it feels funny, but I couldn't see how a long empty corridor full of lockers, all squeezing in on you, how that could be
the right place. I didn't know how I'd react.

When I got to school it was snowing even heavier. I remember
I liked the way the flakes kind of slanted down soft across the sky.
And that made me panic more, the fact that I even noticed the
flakes kind of slanting down soft across the sky. It's not the kind of
thing I usually notice.

In the doorway was the principal, Mr. Babcock. Everyone calls
him "Stump." He's about five feet tall and has no neck, none at all.
When he saw me, he came over and hugged me. He said he was
sorry to learn about my stepfather. I didn't bother to tell him
the difference. I never bother to tell anyone the difference. It's not
that important.

Like I was afraid of, the corridor ahead was long and empty. I
felt it begin to squeeze. Walking down, it got real narrow. Quiet,
too. I had to go way to the other end, and I could hear these thin
voices of teachers who talked faraway. Only my footsteps were
loud. They were pounding off the walls. No matter how light I
stepped, they kept pounding off the walls.

Half way down I turned into the bathroom. In there, some
kids had broken the padlocks and the chains to get at the toilet
paper rolls. Toilet paper streamed from one end of the bathroom
to the other. I was hoping there'd still be a mirror left, because if
I looked the way I felt, then I knew I'd better turn around and go
back home. But the last one had been busted, was already taken
down. There was one tiny piece left, but I could only see my nose
and my mouth a bit in it, or like an eye and a piece of my cheek,

but not the whole face. Every year the school starts with three big mirrors, but usually by the end of second term they're gone, along with a couple of the windows.

In the afternoon I have a study hall, then Algebra II, then French. I was on my way to Algebra II. Mr. Chamberlain is the teacher, Howard Chamberlain. He's taught in the same room for thirty seven years. A couple of years ago, I had him for Algebra I. And every day, from September through June, he wears the same brown sportcoat with the same brown pants and the same brown shoes.

Long before I got to the room, I heard all the noise. No one ever pays attention in Mr. Chamberlain's class. He never seems to care, either. He stands up there, at his overhead, and goes over the homework equation by equation. His voice is real weak to begin with, monotone, but nobody ever pays attention. They eat, or play cards, or sleep, or scream back and forth across the room, but nobody ever does algebra. When he gives us a test, everybody gets about a thirty, but then he scales them up so everybody can pass. It's a great class.

When I walked in, Mr. Chamberlain didn't even look up. He was bent over going real real slow like he does, working his way through a quadratic equation. On the overhead, his marker just barely squeaked across the glass. Jason was half asleep, trying to get through his English homework before seventh period. When he saw me, he pointed and laughed. A couple of the guys next to him pointed and laughed, too. But that's the way it is with Jason, he can't keep anything to himself. That's why I'm worried about what we did now, about us putting it in my locker. Even though he probably won't tell, with him you never know. That's why I'm starting to worry.

I no more than took my seat, and opened my algebra book, when the bell rang. In the doorway Jason acted stoned to get me to laugh, but I didn't. Amanda was out there waiting. I don't laugh too much when Amanda's around, I don't think. I just get kind of uptight. Amanda is my girlfriend. Or at least that's what everyone calls her because I go out with her, so I do too. But it never feels like that. She was in the hall dressed in her cheerleader uniform. Jason was froze there staring at her tits, as usual. She asked me why I didn't call last night. She's always asking me why I didn't do things. I didn't call her because I can't stand to talk to her, can't stand to hear her voice, but I didn't say that though. I just shrugged my shoulders. She got mad, but unless she's getting her own way or surrounding you with those tits of hers, she always gets mad. She stormed off, saying she'd see me after the game. Jason wanted me to go to my locker and get it out, right then and there. He said he'd be waiting in the car. But I didn't want to. I should have, I know, but it was like I couldn't be bothered. Even if it's important, sometimes I just can't be bothered.

Then I had to go to French class. And going to French after algebra is no easy job. Forty minutes with Howard Chamberlain don't exactly get you ready for Madame Bouchard. She's taught at the high school for like thirty-seven years too, but she runs around with her eyes bugging out. Everyone says she's on crack. We all call her "Madame Anal." The minute you walk in the door she's speaking French, so fast no one can understand. She always purses her lips and wears these faggoty-looking French berets and scarves. Mr. Chamberlain's only got one poster in his room, this ripped and faded thing of the first man walking on the moon, but Madame Bouchard's got French flags and pictures of chateaux, and what she calls "cafés romantiques," plastered all over the walls. It's pretty stupid looking. And for forty minutes in there it's nonstop. You can't close your eyes. You can't talk to anyone. You can't think about nothing but French. It's intense. If you doze off, she comes up and slaps her hands together right in front of your face. Then she asks you the last question, as if you can somehow know, and in the quiet everyone laughs. It's stupid. Everyone fucking hates her. Every single second she has to be in control.

After school, the team met for a few minutes in the gym. We always go over a few things with Coach the afternoon of a game. I tried to avoid him. I've never talked to my coach stoned before. He asked me if I was all set to go. I tried not to talk. It's not something I do too much, talk, but it took all I had not to. Then, when everyone was leaving the gym, I asked Coach Higgins if I could just stay in there and shoot around for a while by myself. He thought it was a great idea, a great stress reliever, he said, as long as I took it easy. Jimmy and Nate thought I was crazy. They wanted me to walk over to the mall and get something to eat. And I didn't have to really, but I said I had to be home soon.

I love to shoot around in an empty gym. I always have. There's just something about it. There's this empty echo, it's dark and big, and you're in there alone making up in your mind anything you want to. And you can hear the swish. I love that, too. The swish and the snap. All alone is when I work on things, when I play against imaginary people. I used to make believe I was a pro in the NBA, going against Michael Jordan, or Charles Barkley, players like that. That got pretty intense, but it's not quite like that now. I don't get so intense, disappear like that maybe. It's more quiet. I just go over and over what I know I don't do so good, and I like it almost as much, I think. Like my jump shot, for example. I've always shot it too hard, with not enough touch. I never could figure out why. But now I realize that I was shooting it either going up in the jump, or at the top. That way, my body was just pumping in too much power. Now I realize that the trick is to extend your arms, and to shoot just barely after you start your drop. That way, all that's left to shoot is the wrist. When I can do it, it works great. If it's not clean in, it always stays soft upon the rim. It's not easy to do, though, not easy at all. I can do four or five in a row, that's all, because by then I think too much and go back to my old self. That's why you have to get alone sometimes, and go over and over until there's just no old self to go back to.

Some people say I'm the best player on the team. Some even say in the state. If you look at rebounds and scoring, I suppose what they say could be true. But it hardly ever feels like that. And Coach sure won't let it, either.

By the time I left the gym it wasn't snowing any more. The trees were covered in white, and the sky was already dark. It was a lot colder, too. My house is about twenty minutes from the school. I had to be back by six o'clock, so I wouldn't have much time to fool around once I got there. My house sets back up in a grove of woods with other houses. There's just enough woods so that, in the summer at least, everyone can just barely see each other. The houses are all expensive, at least for around here. Most of the people are what my mother calls "professionals."

When I got home, my mother wasn't there. But she's hardly ever there when I get home. She's either working or doing something else. To get in, I don't have a key. Last year Sidney had this real expensive security system put in, the state of the art, he called it. Instead of using a key, you punch in a code on this panel to open the door. It works every time, but there's a whole series of numbers to remember. At the beginning, I kept forgetting the last number. I had to pry open the garage door and stay in there until one of them came home. Then, a couple of weeks ago, we had this massive ice storm where we lost the power for four whole days. No one could get in the house. Sidney wouldn't let us break a window, they're too expensive, so we had to spend four days in a hotel. Or at least Mom and I did. Sidney stayed at his office. I didn't mind it. There was no school, it was called off, but for four days in a row I had to put on the same underwear. That's the part I remember the most. I'd already gone for two or three days in a row, plenty of times, but by the fourth day they smell pretty ripe.

On the other side of the door I could hear Gretchen. She was crying and whimpering like she does, happy to see me. Gretchen's my dog. She's a collie that we've had ever since I was little. She's eleven years old now, seventy-seven if you count in human years, so she's pretty old. My mother says she's a prize collie with all the papers. She still tells people how she paid over a thousand dollars for her when she was a puppy. We got her when we lived with my stepfather, Harry. He was a pretty cool guy. We lived in this log cabin with a wood stove, and we drove around in an old Jeep. I don't remember all that much, I was just little, but it wasn't bad. He still lives there, but Mom doesn't ever call him. She's not the same, anyway. She always says now that living in the woods like some hippy is fine and dandy if that's all you have to do with your life.

When I opened the door, Gretchen jumped up to lick me. She doesn't jump up like she used to. The vet says she's got arthritis in her hips, so I bend over now and she puts her paws on my thighs and licks my face. She always takes advantage of being up there too, and goes into these nice long stretches. And I know it sounds stupid, but I really like the feel of her tongue on my face, or on my hands. She's always so happy to see me. She's always so happy to see everybody. Even Sidney. Even my mother. And I don't get it. They don't pay hardly any attention to her any more, but, every single time, Gretchen still goes to the door as happy as can be and wags her tail, and waits, as if she expects them to. Every time still, day after day, and I just don't get it.

The first thing I do when I go into the house is turn up the heat. Mom keeps it cold because of this skin problem she thinks she has. She's seen a ton of doctors for it. Now, I think she said she's seeing a laser acupuncturist, whatever that is. The cleaning woman had been in earlier in the day, and the kitchen was spotless. My mother has her come in three times a week. She's Vietnamese or Cambodian or something. She hardly ever says a word. She's nice, but when she talks she like looks at your chest and always has this same strange little smile. She can't say my name, either, and calls me Mister Phirrip. But she's really pretty nice.

I was starved. After school I'm always starved. All the time I'm always starved. It's weird. I looked into the freezer. We have this big freezer that takes up one half of the fridge. When Mom's not home, that's where I get my supper. She tries to be home more, I think, but she's just got so much to do. She's a developmental counselor. She helps little kids to try and adjust. If she's not still at work, she's got like yoga on Tuesday nights, therapy on Wednesday nights, and this holistic medicine something on Thursday nights. Her whole week's like that. But she keeps the freezer full of good stuff, though. I can't complain. There's just about every kind of meal in there you can think of: Mexican, Italian, Indian, everything. All I have to do is pop it in the microwave, and a few minutes later it's done. So it's not all that bad. I mean, some of my friends can't wait to get over here and rifle through my freezer. They don't have food like that at their house, so in a way I'm pretty lucky. She used to make an effort to be here, I remember that, especially on the weekends, so we could have a sit-down dinner. But with just me and her in this big kitchen it was kind of strange. We just don't talk that much anymore. And it's mostly my fault. I really don't want to. I mean, I used to run in and couldn't wait to share stuff with her, but it isn't like that now. And when we sit alone together and she tries to make conversation, tries to get me to talk, it's just sounds too phony.

I grabbed two vegetarian lasagna dinners from the freezer and stuck them in the microwave. Mom doesn't keep red meat in the house. She says red meat is a killer. So everything is vegetarian. "You're never too young to worry about taking care of your body, Philip." Sometimes, though, I have to eat like four frozen vegetarian dinners just so I'm not hungry anymore. It's pretty ridiculous at times. Luckily though, there's a Burger King right next to the school.

The bell rang. Gretchen lifted her head and started to lick her chops. The dinners were ready. I went over and took them out of the microwave, tore off the top paper, and set them on a place mat. Sometimes I get a plate out, but it's easier to eat them right from the containers. That way there's nothing to clean up. I poured myself a big glass of orange juice and sat at the table. I turned on the little TV that sits at the other end. I switched it to ESPN. They were showing *The Miracle Mets*, some old film about a World Series that happened a long time ago. I'd seen it before, but I watched it again. Gretchen came over and put her head on my thigh like she does, looking up at me. I really like it when she does that, when I'm watching TV or eating. She doesn't owe me a thing, and she always looks up at me as if I'm just about the greatest person there is. And when I pat her and talk to her, she just loves that. The least little bit of attention, even if she's busy doing something else, and she just loves it.

After I ate, I went down to the den. I never go down to the den. The den is where Sidney goes. His territory, my mother calls it. In it he's got this 47-inch TV screen that he must have paid thousands for. It's connected to his computer and all this other multimedia stuff, and on the floor are these four massive black speakers.

On the way down I thought of sitting on his couch, turning on his TV, and beating off. But I always think of beating off. That's nothing new. And when I turned on Sidney's TV it was on the

Playboy Channel. Some girl was up there just beginning to lick the ass of another girl, and I had to turn it off. I had to. It's weird, but once I get hard I have to finish. Always. So I just turned it off. I mean I tried that once. I beat off just before a game, earlier in the year, and it was a real horror show. It wasn't until the end of the third period before I could do anything right. I had no legs, no desire, no nothing. And Coach kept screaming at me, right up in my face screaming during the time-outs, but there was nothing I could do. So I won't go beating off before a game again. You can bet on that. I don't care what's on the TV. We lost to a real rotten team that night. And after, I felt so bad I almost went up and told Coach what had really happened, but I guess I'm glad I didn't.

The phone rang. It was Mom. She asked me where I was. I told her in the kitchen. She asked me if I got her e-mail. I told her I hadn't checked the e-mail yet. She said she sent one wishing me good luck in the big game tonight. She said she'd do her best to try and make it, but that with the wake and all she was on a really tight schedule, and I knew how that was. She fully realized how important it was for her to be there though, she said, she wanted me to know how fully she realized that, so she'd try her best, but might not get there till late. Then she wished me luck again and told me she loved me. She always makes it a point to say that she loves me, and to have me say it back. She says her parents never said it to her and that not enough people do, that verbally expressing affection is vitally important on a relational level.

Inside, inside of me I mean, I guess I hoped she'd come to the game. The other kids' parents always come, and when she's there it's different. I always see her, and with all that's going on around me I don't know how, but I always find her, and something just becomes more solid inside and I play even better. I can't explain it. She's only been able to come twice this year so far, but that's good in a way maybe because when she isn't there I don't play like I miss her. I really don't. No one would ever know the difference.

I went upstairs to my room and turned on my computer. I read my mother's e-mail. A big GOOD LUCK! was on a page, surrounded by computerized graphics of balloons and fireworks. Then I was gonna go on the Net, but I realized I didn't have the time, and so I played Doom II instead. It's a stupid game. It really is. I know all the invincibility codes too, so I can't really lose. But it's something to do. I remember it was real fun when I first got it though, trying to blast everybody before they blasted you. I was on it for hours at a time. Now, instead of choosing the plasma gun so I can just annihilate everyone in sight, I choose the chainsaw. That way, I have to run right up on them and gouge them to death. That way too they can kill me off pretty easy, and it's a lot harder to win.

Jason called again. He said that after the game tonight would be a perfect time to get it out. I don't know what I said, but I hung up right away. I didn't want to think about it, not then, not before a game. He's getting to be a real pain in the ass sometimes.

I played Doom II for a few more minutes, and then it was already close to five-thirty. I said goodbye to Gretchen and started walking back to the high school. It was pitch dark out, getting real cold. The snow sparkled fresh and white under the street-lights. The sidewalk had just been plowed. I was only a couple of minutes away from the house when a car honked and stopped just ahead. It was Jimmy's father. In the car was Jimmy and Charley Brooks, the team manager. Jimmy's our center. He's a big guy. He plays tackle on the football team. Him and me are about the same height, but he's a lot wider and heavier. He's great as a pick when you go inside. He don't even have to move. He don't even know he's doing it. He just stands there, and no one can get around him. I always look to see where he is when I take it inside.

Jimmy's father had his head stuck out the car window. I could see his breath. He yelled something about how it was too cold out for our star player to be walking, and to get my valuable ass on in the car. He's pretty funny, Jimmy's father. He keeps you laughing all the time. He drove us up to the high school. He was excited about the game and talking a mile a minute. He always gets excited. He wears his old high school Letter sweater to every game. I see him screaming, jumping up and down over there in the bleachers on every play.

We drove around back and went in through the locker-room door. Everyone inside was quiet. Before a game, Coach wants it quiet. No one jokes, no one talks. Usually we manage to a little, but this time everyone was dead quiet, nervous. That made me realize what was coming up in an hour or so. It would be our toughest game of the year. I knew the guy who would be guarding me too, and he was pretty good, good and a real asshole. I'm not very aggressive as a person I don't think, at least that's what Coach always tells me, but I knew I would have to be with this guy. This guy was a real asshole.

We changed into our uniforms, and then Coach called us into the training room for our pregame meeting. It was then I realized I was still a little stoned from the morning. That surprised me. Coach was going over the game plan on the board, moving the players around, and my eyes kind of settled on things and hung there, not really paying attention. Then, when we went out for warmups, I realized it again too. I mean when I went up for a lay-up, I just kind of hung there a bit longer in the air. It felt pretty strange.

The place was packed, right up to the brim. It was already hot in there, and everybody was standing and cheering so much that the bleachers were rocking back and forth. And I really like that feeling, when I leave a quiet locker room and go running down a line of cheerleaders right straight into all of that. Warmups went great. I don't know if it was the dope or what, I don't think so, but I was loose and nothing else existed but me and that rim. And I was getting nervous. Just at the right time I was getting nervous. When that buzzer went off to end the warmups, no joke, I felt like I could jump right up through that fucking ceiling.

Coach was real nervous. Sweat was pouring down his forehead already. He was speaking fast, babbling almost, trying to go over everything he'd ever taught us, plays, formations, everything in about two minutes. When he gets like that, we all just stand there and nod, as if we understand him perfectly. Then the game buzzer sounded. Waiting out at center court was the guy who'd be guarding me. And he was pretty scary looking. He had like this one big black eyebrow across his forehead, these big hairy shoulders, and his eyes just glared at me. A real asshole. It was clear what his job was too. He'd probably score about two points all night, but that didn't matter, because he was there for one thing and one thing only: to see if he could ram the ball down my stupid throat. And he started in trash talking the second I shook his hand, under his breath so the refs couldn't hear him. He called me a fucking asshole this and a skinny little fucking faggot that. I was nervous. I didn't know how good he was, but he was pretty funny though. He was really good at it.

And when the game started this guy was right in my face. He was quick, quick on his feet, and he always kept them planted. It's an awful feeling, to know what you can do and to have somebody there stopping you from doing it. I hardly ever panic I don't think, but what I felt for those first few minutes was probably close. I mean I started to see the whole game going like that. Then the guy began telling me to go to my left. Go ahead, he kept saying, go to your left you fucking faggot, as if someone had told him I couldn't go to my left. I even saw him starting to favor me a bit on the right. I could've just gone to my left then I suppose, and done okay, but the guy really was just too quick, he wasn't overplaying me enough yet. So then, and don't ask me why, but on a couple of possessions I switched the ball to my left hand and acted like I was bouncing a beach ball. Really, don't ask me why. It's just something that came into my head. The guy even stole it from me once, went the length of the court for a lay-up, and then came back laughing. Coach screamed for a time-out, and shit, did he ever lay into me. He asked me just what to Christ did I think I was doing out there?! Just what?! I told him I thought I had things under control. He just stared at me when I said that, I usually never say a word. Then he screamed just what was that supposed to mean, under christly control?! I didn't say anything. When the time-out was over, he grabbed me by an arm as I was running back out and pulled me in. He rubbed a hand over my hair like he does when he's calmed himself down, and then told me I was a hundred times better than this guy, to just keep working on him because I was a hundred times better.

By now the guy was favoring me way to the right. He couldn't help it. So the next time I touched the ball, I just wheeled it to the left and blew right by him. And I don't often dunk it, but this time I did. I usually just lay it soft off the glass, but this time I dunked it. And with my left hand too. Just to make the point. I heard the crowd go wild. I mean it must've looked pretty awesome. And the guy just kind of growled how I was lucky. But he started inching back towards the middle a bit though. Then I scored twice more on him, driving to the left, and when my right side opened up, I knew I had him. He was back off me a good three or four feet now, with his feet starting to get nervous, and when his mouth finally shut up I really knew I had him. By the middle of the third period his coach was the one screaming. We were about twelve or thirteen points ahead when they dropped the man-to-man and went into this real weak-looking zone. They were way too small for a zone, and so for me it was stay at fifteen to twenty feet time and practice the new form on my jump shot. But no shit, for a while there it was scary.

After the game, some of the guys invited me to go with 'em over to Charlie's house. I guess his parents were gone for the weekend. They always leave a shitload of beer hanging around. I don't drink really, but I go over sometimes and we all scream and holler and play cards. But I couldn't go because I knew Amanda was waiting for me out in the gym. I took my time in the shower, then took my time getting dressed. To tell the truth, I can't stand to see her unless I'm horny. Of course, even if I don't happen to be, she can get me there in like no time flat, so I guess in a way you can say I don't mind seeing her. But then it's like I always hate myself for it. And I just don't get it. The guys keep telling me how lucky I am, and I know I must be, so I just don't get it.

The gym was dark and empty already. Amanda stood out on the floor still dressed in her cheerleader uniform. Her hands were on her hips and she was pissed right off, asking me why I didn't get dressed on time for a change. Like I said, she's always asking me why I didn't do something. She said we were meeting a bunch of cheerleaders over at Burger King, and then going to Kristen Baker's house for a party. We went out to her car, and for about ten minutes then she didn't talk to me. Every time I see her though, there's always about ten minutes where she don't talk to me, where she's pissed off about something I did or didn't do. Sometimes I think she almost like senses the way I really feel, and don't know how else to react. But after about ten minutes she always grabs my arm and begins snuggling in real close with those big soft tits of hers, and, what can I say, everything changes.

Burger King was too loud and too bright. I don't know why. It never is. I was too tired I guess. I never get tired either, but it was a long hard game and I felt really tired. All the cheerleaders were there with their boyfriends. Their faces lit up too when they saw me walk in. They all told me what a great game I played. That felt pretty good. Then they all got up to go to their party. I really didn't want to go. I always go too, even when I don't want to, but this time I just couldn't. I don't know why. I told Amanda I didn't think I was going, that I felt sick. I figured, how could she be mad at me if I told her I was sick? But of course I figured wrong. Her face just turned beet red. She was really embarrassed. And everyone begged me to go but I just couldn't. When they all left, Amanda just stood there, on the verge of tears, asking me if I was coming or not. When I said I couldn't, that I didn't feel good, she just turned and ran out the door. And I hate it when that happens. I mean emotion like that that I'm somehow the cause of, when you're only just being yourself and that you're somehow the cause of, when only a lie can make things better.

I walked home from Burger King. It was real cold out. The wind was blowing hard, but it felt good. The air felt good. The lights were on in the house, but when no one's home at night the lights always go on. That's part of the security system, so you really never know if someone's home or not. Gretchen met me at the door. And no one was home. Mom had left a note on the kitchen table. She congratulated me for the great game and told me she'd gone out for a drink with some of Sidney's friends, and for me to just grab something to eat or watch TV and then go on to bed, that she'd probably not be home until late. I was starved. I went into the freezer, took out two black bean enchilada dinners, and stuck them in the microwave. I sat at the table waiting for the buzzer and turned on the kitchen TV. It was still on ESPN. The program was car racing, an old Daytona 500, and I hate car racing but watched it anyway. The buzzer sounded. I turned off the TV, put the two plastic dishes on a tray, then poured myself a glass of milk. When I started to walk up the stairs, Gretchen stayed at the bottom crying and wagging her tail, looking up at me. Ma don't want her upstairs, and she has a hard time getting up even when she's allowed, because of her arthritis. I set my tray on the landing, and then went back down and carried Gretchen up, getting all kinds of big warm sloppy kisses on my face for providing the help.

In my room, I sat on the bed and ate. I put on my earphones. They're these special German earphones that Sidney bought me once. They cost over four hundred bucks. They've got like this wave technology that goes from ear to ear, and that's supposed to make music even better than it really is, I mean in real life. After I ate, I went over to the computer, put in a CD-ROM and tried to play Mega-Death, this game my uncle Tommy bought me for Christmas, but I was just too tired. You've really got to get into it, get on edge and get your nerves going, or you get slaughtered right off. I just didn't have the energy.

I turned on the TV. I flicked for a while, went through all the thirty-five channels, but nothing was on. Then I didn't feel at all like beating off, but did anyway. I don't think I thought of anything either. I just did it. Then I lifted Gretchen up on the bed so she could sleep beside me. I knew Mom would be furious. Gretchen stretched way out beside me and rolled up on her back, looking at me like she does, just waiting for me to run my hand up and down over her tummy. She really likes that. Then I turned out the light and just laid there. I looked up into the black, thinking about how I wheeled it to the left past that asshole and dunked it. Then I went over a few practice jump shots in my mind. I could feel Gretchen beside me, her weight like warm and soft down the length of me all cuddled in close. And I know it's stupid, but I like that, I mean feeling her weight there beside me when I go to sleep. I don't know why, but it's really pretty cool.

saturday > > >

I woke up with a hard-on. But that's nothing new. I always wake up with a hard-on. That's just the way it is. Jason does too. And I was having this dream I remember. I was sunk in something warm. I was in this real deep warm liquid, watching this woman dressed in white, all dressed in this soft and like waving see-through white. She had these huge brown nipples. I remember that. She motioned to me, with this nice warm smile, and I moved, don't ask me how, but I was like gliding slowly in between her thighs. It was definitely intense. I tried to do it right then and there, I mean when it was hard, inside of that floating and warm, trying to continue the feeling right on into real life. But you never can. There's a wall. It's just not the same kind of hard. There's two kinds. It takes a while to realize that. I used to think they were the same, but once you touch it, it's like the whole thing stops, you wake up, and the world comes in. Everything warm goes. And you have to like let it shrink back down, then start all over again from nothing if you want to do it. But it's never the same. Whatever you had is gone.

I began doing it anyway though. I mean I usually do. And I thought of Mrs. Jenkins. If I don't have a picture or a monitor in front of me, I always think of Mrs. Jenkins. She was my sophomore English teacher. She always wore red, red and black. When

I think of her I see a tight black skirt, these thick red lips, and this tight red sweater that shows her nipples. Pizza face, that's what everyone at school calls her, but she wears like these tall black high heels. None of the other teachers ever dress like that. She used to sit on her desk and cross her legs. One high heel kind of dangled off her foot and she talked about Huckleberry Finn, or the Mayor of Casterbridge, and no joke, some days it really got to me. No joke. And to all the other guys too. I don't know why. But she has this way of looking at you, of laughing deep down in her throat. And so in my mind I have to stay after school one afternoon. She's sitting in front of me on the desk, and somehow I touch her by mistake I think. And she reacts. She loves it. And those big red lips of hers kind of open. Then I take my hand and move it real real slow up her thigh, and then she like . . .

but this is all so fucking stupid. It is. I don't know why I do it. This is really so fucking stupid.

Right in the middle, Mom knocked on the door. She didn't come in. She didn't have to. Mrs. Jenkins disappeared. My mother never comes in. She did a couple of years ago and caught me. She was more embarrassed than me I think. But I was pretty embarrassed. She mentioned it a few days after, trying to laugh, down in the kitchen. She said she just wanted me to know that as far as she was concerned, it was merely a form of self-expression, that I needn't at all feel ashamed. I wish she'd never said that though. For a long time after, every time I touched it, the word "self-expression" came like flashing through my brain. It didn't help matters any.

Through the door, my mother said she was going out for coffee. She said she'd be back around noon. Then she congratulated me on the game again, and turned away from the door. I heard her steps go down the stairs. They started real loud and ended up almost far away. A couple of minutes later I heard the door shut.

Gretchen was still stretched out beside me. My mother hadn't gotten mad, hadn't stormed in to get Gretchen, and that surprised me. And Gretchen too. At first she was all coiled up staring at the door, and then, when the steps went away, she just looked up at me and rolled over on her back like she does, wagging her tail and spreading her hind legs, waiting for my hand to rub up and down her tummy.

I stayed in bed. I was starved. But I stayed in bed. On Saturday morning I like to do that, just lay under the covers and kind of stare, half asleep, thinking of my life and stuff. Everything seems real clear then, like you can surround it all in one glance. Most of the time it's not like that. Most of the time things are in pieces, all scattered here and there. It's not always easy to pull them in, to make sense of them all at once.

So I stayed under the covers. My room was real quiet. Some bright sun came in through the window and hit a wall. My walls are still crammed with all my old junk. I never throw anything away. I don't know why. Whenever I put something new up I just search and search until I find a place for it. I even still got this old Michael Jackson poster I put up way back in first grade. He's standing there dancing up on his toes, with this one diamond glove held high in the air. His black pants are pulling up over these white socks, and he's grabbing for his balls. It's pretty ridiculous. I'm glad I kept it up there though, 'cause every time Jason comes over we still can't stop laughing at it. Then I got clippings and pictures from a lot of my games up there. That was my mother's idea. I never look at 'em really. Most of the time it's like it's somebody else.

After laying there for a while I flicked on the TV. Yosemite Sam was on, shooting his six-guns and screaming about "massacrein' him a bunch of them varmints." He's pretty cool. Then Pepe LePew came on, this skunk speaking like in French. He was romancing this sexy white cat who fainted from his smell, and so he thought it was because she was madly in love with him. That was pretty funny too. When I was young, I remember I used to watch cartoons all Saturday morning, and then about eleven o'clock just run like mad outside into the day and play.

I shut the TV off and laid back in bed. Gretchen was sound asleep again. I was still starved. Then I heard voices come in from outside, kids' voices. The little kids next door were outside playing in the snow. Then I thought of Cheryl. Or at least I must have. Whenever it's quiet, whenever I like have time by myself, I think of Cheryl. It's just the way it is. Actually, I always think of her, all the time, in behind I mean, but it's when I'm in bed that her face comes in, when I remember the way we talked and stuff. I don't like to. I try not to. And I never beat off to her either. I've tried to a couple of times, and I suppose I could force it if I wanted to, but it's just not the same. There's like this corner I don't want to turn.

I got up. Gretchen didn't want to move. She has this way of like making every muscle go dead until she weighs about a ton, and so I practically had to drag her off the bed before we could go downstairs.

Down in the kitchen, the sun was coming in bright off the new snow. The newspaper was already on the table. That's the first thing I look for, the newspaper, to eat my breakfast with. I got out the milk, the cereal, a bowl, and then turned to the sports section. On the first page was a picture of this boxer, Evander Holyfield. He had this big bloody bite taken out of his ear. I couldn't believe it. Then I read the article. It said how Mike Tyson had bitten him twice, had taken this big chunk out of Holyfield's ear. I laughed and laughed I remember. Then, when I turned to the next page, there I was. It was a big picture too, full length. The guy'd taken it from under the basket, just when I was making that dunk. There's this real nasty snarl on my face, mean, and the ball's kind of like whipping down through the net. Way in the background, asshole's just standing there in the middle of the court with this shit-eaten grin on his face. It was a pretty awesome picture. Then I read the article and it said how the team was stymied, I remember thinking I never heard that word before, how the team was stymied for almost a full period until I decided to take things into my own hands and just exploded, putting the game out of reach. And I kind of liked the way they put that.

I ate three or four bowls of cereal, but was still starved. I went over to the freezer, pulled out a sixteen-inch pepperoni and hamburg pizza, one that I'd hidden in the back away from my mother, then stuck it in the microwave. And old Gretchen's ears sure popped up at that. That's her favorite sound, the hum when I hit the start button. I mean next to the little bell at the end of course.

I turned on the kitchen TV. It was still on ESPN. They were showing an old Super Bowl, the Kansas City Chiefs and the Minnesota Vikings playing in the snow. I'd seen it before, plenty of times, but I watched it again. The bell rang. I went and got the pizza, poured myself a glass of milk, then sat and watched the TV. I love to do that too, eat pizza and watch TV. I don't know what it is. Gretchen came over and stood there with her head nuzzled in on my thigh like she does, looking up at me. She knows she won't get nothing until after, but she just likes to watch I guess.

Halfway through the pizza, Jason called. He sounded worried. He was saying that Mike Pooler might have found out, and that today we just had to go into school and take it out of my locker, when no one was around. There was some kind of a band concert going on in the gym too, so we could like slip in easy and take it out before anyone noticed. Then he said how we could get in big trouble, even someone like me, but he'd be the one to get all the real shit, because he usually does. He sounded really worried.

Jason never worries about anything either. I told him I was busy
this afternoon. Then he begged me to go in and try sneaking it
out tonight, but I told him I was busy then too. I told him I
would take it out some night after practice, not to worry. He just
said that if "Stump" ever found out, the police would be all over
that school.

After I finished my pizza, I picked up Gretchen and went back
upstairs. From outside, those kids' voices still came, all happy and
laughing. Through the window I saw them over there sliding in
the snow. I sat down, put on my headset, put a CD in the CD
player, and turned on the computer. I had a big algebra test Monday. I knew if I didn't study a little at a time I'd have a real hard
time with it. Algebra's my worst subject. I work like crazy just to
get a C. It kept me from getting honors twice this year already,
and I'm sure it'll stop me twice more. I don't mind it either. I like
moving all those numbers around, switching them from side to
side and seeing how it works out, but it just makes no sense to
me. I can't see what it's good for. I don't see the point. And when
I can't see what something's good for, I just have a hard time getting it.

My mother helped me with algebra at the beginning of the
year. She's real good at math. I did better there too, but she just
didn't have the time. So she bought me this great algebra software
kit instead. The program itself costs over three hundred and fifty
dollars, so that's how good it is. It lays everything out for you,
and takes you through each equation step by step. This sexy
woman's voice tells you when you're making a mistake too, and
to "rethink that option, please, Philip." But I had a hard time
installing it. I called their 1-800 number and got this menu, then I
chose a new number and got another menu, then I chose another
new number and got another menu, and I never ever did get a
real live voice to talk to. That's all I wanted really. I finally had this

guy I know from school come over and he installed it easy. I was just making the wrong selection.

I used to do real good in school, like high honors all the time. Things came easy to me. But I'm slipping now and I don't know why. Every time my mother sees a report card she just about loses it. She has these visions of me like going to an Ivy League college. She always has, ever since I was little. Last year she even set up these special meetings at school with my teachers. It was pretty embarrassing. None of my teachers could see a problem. They all said I was a great kid, a great student, and a great athlete too. If I seemed to be slipping a little, it was only because I was taking on more. But Mom kept worrying. She even sent me to this guy, this educational psychologist. We had two sessions a week for six months, at 120 dollars a session, and we never did anything except talk about sports. The guy was a real sports fan. Sometimes I tried to talk about school, and the trouble I was beginning to have, but all the guy wanted to talk about was me playing basketball and sports. The Boston Celtics, the New York Yankees, the latest trades, what were my thoughts on a ten-point spread between the Knicks and the Bulls, on seven points between the Lakers and the Sonics. I mean I didn't know. But week after week it was the same old shit, until I hated even going into his office. I just sat there and never said a word.

Come to find out, the guy submitted this form to the school telling them I had A.D.D. That stands for attention deficit disorder. When my mother heard that, she just about flipped. Then she went around telling everyone how she'd always noticed I'd had a hard time paying attention, ever since I was a baby. So now I have to go down to the library twice a week with this guy from Special Ed. He reads to me and I practice paying attention. It's pretty stupid. And everyone in the school goes to the library.

But I am slipping though, I can feel it. Maybe I'm not paying attention as much as before, I don't know, or maybe I'm not as smart as I used to be. Maybe too this whole thing about not paying attention is just how it comes out.

For a few minutes I worked on my algebra. The kids still played outside in the snow. Then, just sitting there doing a quadratic equation, I got hard again. I don't know why. It's just the way it is. I do know that when I have to stop for some reason though, interrupt it, like when my mother knocked on the door, it just kind of sits in you and waits to be finished. I fought it for a few minutes, and then I went on the Net. I got through right away, and I know exactly where to go too so I was on the right page in no time. My friend Jason practically lives there. He'll like dial a 1-900 sex talk number and get this girl talking to him, go on the Net to an adult page, and then get himself off in the middle of all that.

When I got there, The Pix of the Day were of this girl named Lacey. There were ten pictures. In one she was dressed in these white stockings and garters. She was on her knees with her ass to the screen. Her legs were spread wide so you could see her cunt. A couple of the others were not that good. Then there was this real good one where this other girl, Samantha, this blond with these beautiful tits, she was like lapping Lacey's cunt. I went back and forth between those two, I mean for as long as I could. But my fucking system ain't like Jason's though. He's got APG video with textured 3-D pixels. I keep asking my mother to upgrade but she won't. And you can't really do it right, not and concentrate, because things don't stay together the way they should, not when you really begin to stare. The pixels pull apart, and an ass don't even look like an ass after a while, and something like a cunt you always have to end up guessing at. I mean I don't get off like I know I could. I don't. I'm sure of that. I know if I had a better system it would be better. I mean Jason has an LCD monitor with a two-hundred-hertz refresh rate. That's fucking incredible. It sets up 1800 by 1400 pixels. It's like you have the ass and the tits right there with you, like on a real person. You can watch them doing each other, like you're right there. Nothing pulls apart either because the dot pitch is so small, like .12 mm, and so it's like seeing a real picture, I mean like having a real picture right there with you. No shit, things would be just perfect if I only had a system like that.

After, I tried to go back and do quadratic equations. But forget it. I laid down on the bed instead. The kids still played outside. Their voices were small. They jumped up and down in the cold. And I hate to think about sex all the time too. I do. I get so sick of it, of thinking about it, of having it in me all the time. It's like it explodes at times when you don't even want it there, but by then it's too late, it's already there. And when it's gone out of you it leaves you so empty. I just know I should be thinking about other things. I mean I had an algebra test on Monday for chrissakes. And I hate to feel empty.

I slept I think. Then the phone rang. It was Missy. She was the last person I wanted to talk to. Lately, she's always the last person I want to talk to. She's always so negative now. She talks about how she can't take another day, how she's just gonna have to kill herself. I mean you can only feel sorry for so long. Missy is a friend of mine from like way back in first grade. We used to do everything together. I remember us like kissing under the school steps in second grade, and then going out into the field and pulling our pants down, stuff like that. But we were never girl-friend and boyfriend though, just real good friends. Then last year she called me one day. She cried and told me she was preg-nant. She came over, and up in my room she must have cried and cried for hours. She said I was the only person she dared to tell, that no one else could know, not even her boyfriend. She said if he ever found out it would be the end of their relationship, she just knew it would. She couldn't tell her parents either, because they'd make her have the baby and she just couldn't have a baby, not at sixteen, so I was the only person she could trust. I didn't know what to do. But Missy had a plan. Since she was over sixteen, she could go to a clinic for an abortion she said, and legally they couldn't inform her parents without her consent. She begged me to go with her, and to like make believe the baby was mine so she didn't look cheap. She said if I didn't go she would kill herself. I didn't think she would kill herself, but I'd never seen anyone so upset, especially not someone who was always laughing like Missy. She said she'd call and make the appointment, go in for the examination herself, and then all I had to do was go back with her when they did the abortion. I said I would. I mean the whole situation made me feel uneasy, I didn't like it, but Missy had herself so upset that it didn't seem that much to do.

We went on a Thursday after school. We took Missy's mother's car. The appointment was for three-thirty. It was in a town about twenty miles away, so we had to hurry. The building was one of those new low ones, with lots of windows across the front. A blue sign was stuck in the front lawn with this big yellow butterfly on it. It said Women's something Clinic.

Missy was real nervous, crying and nervous. I just felt strange. She told me to remember that I was her boyfriend, that I would probably have papers to sign. She held my hand as we went through these automatic doors. I hoped no one would recognize me from the paper, from me playing basketball. Inside though, everyone was really nice. They were all women, and they all smiled and said hello. They brought us into this room where there was orange juice, doughnuts, and these little kind of sandwich things. We sat there for a few minutes, and then a doctor came out, another woman. She said she had some good news. Missy's pregnancy wasn't quite as far along as they'd thought, and that surgical intervention may not be necessary. She said they had this new pill that was now legal, and that maybe the new pill would do the trick. She wanted Missy to take the pill right then and there, and to stay the night for observation. She said there would be cramps, discomfort, and a discharge too was the word she used. Missy said she couldn't. The nurse asked if we had a safe place we could go. Missy said we did.

If we did have a safe place to go though, I sure didn't know about it. Out in the car, Missy said we'd just have to get a hotel. She rifled through her purse, looking for money. She found twenty-five dollars, including change, that we could put towards a room if we didn't have to buy gas. I had seven. But we were twenty miles away from our town, with the gas gauge on empty, so we had to buy gas. We ended up getting five dollars worth. That left us with twenty-seven dollars. Then we drove along real slow, looking at all the signs out in front of the motels, trying to find one for twenty-seven dollars.

It didn't take us that long to find one. About the third motel was an Econo Lodge. The sign out front read twenty-five dollars. Missy sent me in alone. She said they wouldn't question a guy so much. Behind the counter there was this skinny guy wearing a tie. I was pretty nervous. I handed him the twenty-five dollars and told him I wanted a room. He looked me over real good, then winked and told me, sure thing kid, anything for someone with a jump shot as great as yours. With that, I felt like sliding back out across the floor. Then he winked again, nodded out towards Missy's car, and told me to have a real good time.

The room was in a basement, down this flight of stairs. It was small and dark. One small window was up near the ceiling. It kind of looked out over the top of some grass. I sat on the bed. Missy went right into the bathroom and took the pill. When she came back out, she told me I could put on the television, that she didn't mind. Then I sat on the bed and leaned my back against the wall. I watched the television, but I don't remember what was on. Then Missy started to cry again beside me. She asked me to hold her. We've been friends for practically all our lives, Missy and me, but I'd never held her before, not in my arms, not like girlfriend and boyfriend. I remember I didn't like the feeling too much, but that Missy seemed to want me to, to need me to. Then she began to cry even more, there in my arms. She said she was killing her baby, right at that very second she was killing her baby. I didn't expect that, those words I mean, I'd never thought of it like that. I still don't either I don't think, but I don't know. She was bawl-ing, saying that over and over. I held her. And I remember I felt so cold inside. I couldn't respond. I would've never expected that either. Maybe because there was nothing I could do, or I didn't want to be there, I don't know, but I felt like this cold cold stone inside. And the room was dark with only the TV going. Missy was crying there in my arms. It flickered this hard white light back into our eyes and up over the walls. And I can't even remember what was on.

Then, an hour or two later maybe, she started getting pains in her stomach, cramps. She was like bent right over on the bed. Then she started to throw up and ran into the bathroom. A few minutes later I tried to go in. She was sitting on the toilet and she screamed at me, shaking her head and screaming at me, telling me to get back out. I didn't know what to do. I didn't know what was going on either, I mean not then. Now I do. And I don't know how long she stayed in there, one hour, two, it's hard to say, but I kept on hearing her crying and crying and hearing the toilet flush. Out in the room, I watched the television there in the dark. Its white light flickered back hard into my eyes and up over the walls. Then I heard the shower.

When Missy came out she looked awful. She was as white as a

ghost. She trembled, but she didn't cry any more. Her face had this hard look on it almost. I went to hold her, but she pushed me away. She said she was fine, not to worry about her, that she was fine. She just wanted to get out of there. I said I didn't mind staying until she felt better. She said she couldn't, that she had to be home by eleven o'clock, that if she wasn't home by eleven o'clock on a school night her parents would kill her.

For about two months after, Missy avoided me at school and never once called me. She broke up with her boyfriend too, and I guess he never found out. Then one day she called me all mad. She blamed me for letting her go through with it. It was crazy. She talked about how she hated herself, wanted to kill herself, and how if she did, it would be on my conscience. The first few times I tried to talk to her, but she kept calling like five or six times a day, blaming me and saying this real negative stuff.

Now, at least, I don't think she blames me any more. But she still talks about killing herself, and about how she dreams of her baby every night. I mean I know I'm the only one she can talk to, but I don't want to hear it. It's not my problem. If she didn't want to do it, then she shouldn't have done it in the first place. It's just not my fucking problem.

After she hung up, I grabbed the basketball and headed outside on the porch for a minute. It's funny, but the minute I just have it there on my hip things feel better. Ever since like second or third grade I've had a basketball with me everywhere I go, dribbling up and down the sidewalks. Next door, the kids screamed and laughed in the snow. I saw their breaths rise in the air. And the guy who blew out the driveway was down at the end, just starting up. A big fan of white spread out high, throwing this powder across the blue. When I was little I used to love to play outside in the snow too. I remember I used to love to fall down all out of breath and just lay there, looking up into the sky, feeling like I was falling up into it, the air so cold on my face like ice. There was just something about it.

When I went back in the house, Amanda had called and left a message. Her voice was changed from the night before, all soft and sexy. I knew it would be. She said her parents would be gone for the entire day, that if I wanted to come over we would have the whole house to ourselves. At that very second I didn't, it was the last thing I wanted, but I knew that after an hour of quadratic equations, and listening to the playback of her voice, I'd probably be out on the sidewalk dribbling my way over.

I don't get this thing between Amanda and me. I don't. It's not what you'd call normal. I mean I'm rotten to her most of the time and she puts up with it. Every guy in the school wants to go out with her too. All they can talk about, all they ask me about, is her tits. No joke. Every guy in the school tries to imagine what they're like. So I know I should consider myself lucky. And they really are something else. They're like you see in a magazine. And the first time I saw them I tried not to stare. I mean I didn't want her to think I was going out with her just for her tits, but it was hard not to. That's why I don't understand how they could go from what they were then, to what they are now. Sometimes now they're just these big fat jugs. I don't get it. I hate it. Then I'll wait a week or two, see her, and they'll be beautiful again. So I just don't get it.

And her breath. No shit. Her breath is just so rancid at times. It's hard to describe. I don't know if it's the braces or not, but all I can think of is like a mixture of pickles and rusting metal, like pickles and these rusty tin cans. It's not all that easy to get past. And when we do it, she never stops talking. She always asks how it feels, if I love her, if I like her body. We might as well be doing it over the phone. And it's okay, but it's not how I thought it would be. And then when it's over, Jesus, when it's over is a real disaster. In me I mean. She stays right up where she was, and I'm like way down here somewhere. She's still pawing at me, breathing all over me, so I have to try and make believe, and keep plugging away as best I can. Then she lays there all content and starts in talking about the future. She talks about us maybe getting married some day, about us having kids. Honest, laying there when it's over is a real horror show.

Like I said, after an hour of doing quadratic equations, and hearing her voice on the answering machine, I grabbed my basketball and began to dribble my way over.

When I finally left Amanda's, about six o'clock, I was pretty exhausted. All I wanted was to go home, eat, and get some sleep. Amanda wanted me to stay. She said she'd make me a nice supper, and then we could sit on the couch together and watch a movie until late. I told her I had an algebra test. She said I had all day Sunday to study. I said I know, but that algebra was something I had to study a lot. She got mad at that. She said I didn't care at all about spending time with her. I said I did. She said I didn't. I said I did. Then she turned away and wouldn't talk to me. But I wasn't surprised. I don't think I've ever left her yet when she was still talking to me. But it's my fault, I know that. I sat on the couch for about an hour then. I hoped she'd think that I was like too torn to leave her, that I really didn't want to. I don't think I quite pulled it off though. When I left she was still sitting quiet on the couch, on the verge of tears.

It felt great to get back outside, to finally breathe some fresh air again. It was night. The air was good and cold. The fresh snow creaked as I walked. And as usual, like I always do when I leave Amanda, I felt rotten for quite a while.

Gretchen met me at the door. Mom was just on her way out to have dinner with some friends. She said she'd made me a nice supper, all I had to do was heat it up. When I went into the kitchen I saw it was my favorite, tuna casserole. She makes it with cans of organic cream of mushroom soup, organic macaroni, and peas and carrots. I eat it with like loads of ketchup and cranberry sauce. A huge pan of it was on the kitchen table, enough for two or three nights probably. But I was starved. I was too hungry to warm it up, so I just ate it right from the pan, the whole thing, watching some college game on ESPN.

Then, after I ate, this big wave of being tired came over me. I carried Gretchen up the stairs, went into my room, and laid down on the bed. I turned on the TV. Some dumb movie was on. It was one of those Chinese karate movies. The hero guy was like spinning around kicking in circles, and all these other guys were falling down, even though they were about a mile away from his feet. It was pretty stupid.

Then I slept I think. And I hate that, when I go to sleep too early, still all dressed. You feel like a scuz when you wake up. I could tell it was a lot later. I heard Mom downstairs, so I knew it had to be around midnight. The TV was still on. I flicked it off, and went into the bathroom to brush my teeth. When I came back out, I realized Gretchen was still on the bed. Mom hadn't even come up the stairs to get her. I had no clue why.

I tried to sleep but couldn't, so I just laid there. I thought of Cheryl. Like I said, when I lay in bed I always think of Cheryl. Sometimes I let it come, sometimes I don't. I guess that night I let it come.

I went with Cheryl my whole sophomore year. On a dare once from some of her friends, she asked me to dance at a school dance. And right from that second, I mean the second we danced, the second we looked at each other, everything around us changed. There's no way I can describe it. It was like we shared some kind of a secret.

After the dance we started seeing each other, going out. And every single time together we had the same feeling. I liked everything about her, her hair, her teeth, her breath, the way her voice sounded. It was strange. She was from Worthington, and I'd bike out there and we'd like walk from her house down to the lake to go skating. And I would just change when I was with her. I even sang I remember. No joke. I would walk along singing these songs when I can't even carry a tune. She'd just look at me and laugh and laugh. Each time I left her, I couldn't wait to see her again. It was really strange, like something hurt deep inside and wouldn't let up until I did. And we never said anything about the future, about plans, about love, at least not like everyone else does. We didn't dare to I don't think. It was like it was too good almost, like we didn't want to jinx it.

Then one day at the end of our sophomore year she came up to me in school. I could see she was really upset. She told me her parents had decided that we shouldn't date any more, that we were too involved for kids our age. Most kids I know wouldn't listen to that, they'd just keep on seeing each other during school or out somewheres else, but Cheryl really respects her parents, and so I knew when she said it she meant it. She said she couldn't go to the last dance of the year with me either, that she had to accept an invitation from someone else. Then she looked at me and told me she loved me. She'd never told me that before. Then she turned and ran crying down the hallway.

I had to go into French class. I'll never forget that. I was like lost, numb. It took a while for it to hit me, and then I started to cry, I mean right there in French class, right there in front of everybody. I cried just like a baby, me of all people. I felt so stupid, but I couldn't stop. Madame Bouchard didn't know what was going on. She sent me out in the hall. I went out and just like stood there against the lockers, empty. Everything was black inside, sucked right out of me. Then Madame Bouchard came out and asked me what was the matter, did something bad happen. I just shook my head. Then she put her arm around me and squeezed. I felt really stupid.

That was over a year ago already. Like I said, Cheryl still never leaves my mind, and I almost think now she never will. I know I'll move on and stuff, like my mother said, but I think she'll always be there in behind. And I almost want her to. I try to keep her out, I know it's better that way, especially when I have things to do. But when she comes back in most of what I feel is warm. I feel sad, I feel real lonely, but if I'm laying in bed with time to bring everything all the way back, her face, her smell, our walks and everything, I mean most of what I feel all around me then is really nice and warm.

sunday > > >

I hate Sundays. Sunday is a real nothing day. My grandparents come over and we go to church. Then we go
to their house for dinner, eat dry roast beef and these
vegetables that turn to shit when they touch your
fork, and then I sit there so bored I want to puke. Sundays suck.

At eight o'clock my mother knocked on my door. Gretchen
was still beside me on the bed. Two nights in a row that made, so
something was up. My mother said Grammy and Grampy would
be here in a half hour, that I had to hurry. But every week it's the
same thing, the same words. And every week too I lay in bed for a
while, listen to a CD, watch some TV, then get up to take a shower
and they're still not here yet.

Unless one of 'em's sick, they come every Sunday. We go to
the ten o'clock worship service at the Brewster Congregational
Church. I went to Boy Scouts in the same church, down in the
basement. I don't go any more, but I was a Scout for a long time.
I went to Scout Camp every summer. I was even an assistant
counselor there my last summer. I took the kids out on hikes and
stuff. In a way I learned a lot in Scouts. I stayed in it until about
halfway through my sophomore year. When I left I was an Eagle
Scout with fifty-four Merit Badges. That's a lot of Merit Badges.
But basketball and studying just started to take up too much

time. And it wasn't the coolest thing to be known as around school either.

My grandparents are pretty old. They're both like sixty something. My grandfather's retired from the papermill. He was what they call a Master Carpenter. Anything at the mill that had to do with wood, him and his team of carpenters were called in to fix it. He's pretty cool, my grandfather. He's got this carpenter shop out in his garage where he still makes chairs and tables, things like that. When I was little I used to go over and spend all day Saturday. I'd just sit there and watch him work. He taught me how to use some of his tools too, even the wood lathe. But when I think back now I can't believe I ever did that, and not get bored, I mean just sit there all day and watch him work.

My grandmother sewed clothes for people. She shortened pants and skirts, stuff like that. She still does. She never had a job outside, I don't think. She's got their house jammed right full of junk too, of souvenirs. Little statues of dogs and cats, and of these smiling little idiot German kids, they're packed in everywhere. She's also got billions of salt and pepper shakers and ashtrays. There's not an inch that's not crammed with something. It all looks like what you win at a fair. My mother hates it. She says it looks tacky. She makes fun of it every time we go over. I don't think they get along all that good, those two. I guess my mother gave them a hard time when she was growing up. My grandmother still says how she was always a rebel, how she left too young to go gallivanting around the country. My grandfather never talks about it much, but he never talks about anything too much. But it's strange to hear Grammy tell those stories about my mother, I mean she's sure nothing like that now.

At Sunday dinner I just sit there. We're never even allowed to turn on the TV. And we always go over there alone. Sidney never once went with us. My grandparents never even mentioned him.

My mother used to like let on to other people it's because he's Jewish, but Grammy and Grampy aren't like that, not at all. And over there my mother changes. She complains all the time. She just picks at her food. She makes these comments, too, where she always begins by saying that she knows how she shouldn't make them, how she hates to make them, but then she makes them anyway. Every week. And always about the same things. The way the vegetables are cooked, about eating red meat, I mean it's stupid. Sometimes I wish she'd just shut up. I don't know why she does it. It hurts my grandmother when she talks like that, I can see it.

When we came home from my grandparents', my mother got her running clothes on and went for a jog. She does that a couple of times a week. She's got this running outfit that costs a fortune I bet. It's made of this matching pink Lycra stuff. She's got these running shoes too that I've seen advertised for like two hundred dollars. She never used to be like that either, but more and more she's getting this thing about how she looks. She's real worried about it. She gets these acid treatments for her face, to remove wrinkles I guess. At least I think that's what it's for because she's always asking me if they're smaller. And just last year she had her breasts fixed. But she's always been real conscious of her breasts. She still tells everyone how one of the worst decisions she ever made in her life was to breast-feed me, that it absolutely ruined her breasts. They weren't very big to begin with I guess, and the way she tells it, me breast-feeding like drained the life right out of them, made 'em just hang there. I've heard some of her friends complain about the same thing too. Then last year she had this operation. She explained the whole thing to me, even though I didn't want to know, about where the incision would be and where the silicon implants would go. I didn't want to hear it, but she said I was mature enough to know. It was a perfectly normal operation for a human being to have, she said, a perfectly useful tool for enhancing self-esteem. It looks okay on her I guess, I mean they're really round, but it just doesn't look like my mother. And she likes it so much that now she's talking about getting what's called a "tummy tuck." I told her I didn't see why she needed anything like that, she's not fat, but she calls it a preventive measure, trying to get there before age does. So I don't know.

I got back home from my grandparents' about three-thirty. Amanda had called and left a message. She said her parents would be gone all day again. I didn't call back. I really had to study for my algebra test. I need time. I'm a person who has to write everything down when I study. If I don't, it just won't sink into my stupid head. I had an 83 average going this term in algebra, my highest ever, only two points away from a B, and maybe High Honors, so I didn't want to blow it.

Outside, the kids played in the snow again. I put a CD in the player and put on my headset. The kids disappeared. Then I opened my algebra book. Quadratic equations. The quadratic formula. Absolute boring shit. Jesus. I mean how much fun can one person stand?!

Later, I felt a hard tap on my shoulder. Mom stood there. I took off my headset. She told me she'd been knocking on the damn door, screaming her damn lungs out, and that I was going to go deaf having that damn headset so loud. It wasn't the first time I'd heard that. I had a phone call, from my biological father, she said. That's what she calls him, my biological father. I went downstairs to the phone. Like always, he was a bit nervous. He tries to be cool, funny. My mother thinks he's pretty screwed up. I do too, at least in a way, but not in the way she thinks.

They met when my mother was in graduate school. When I was younger my mother made me sit down and listen to the whole story. She said she wanted me to know the truth about my existence, the how and why of my conception, that it was vitally important for my psychological growth.

He was a few years older than she was. She was working in this veterans' place. I guess she counseled war veterans for credit in some college course, and that's where they met. She was twenty-seven by then, and really wanted to experience birthing and the raising of a child, or at least that's the way she put it. Hormonally, she told me, and she like made a joke I remember, it was definitely time. But in no way was she ready to put the brakes on her life with a marriage. No way. But she liked him. He was at base a good man, a bit screwed up but good, and so she decided to have a child with him. He went along with the idea too I guess, although I don't know if I believe that part so much any more. She still laughs about it with her friends sometimes, about having the foresight to choose a donor with such an excellent gene pool, and about getting a top-notch athlete in the bargain to boot. Everyone always seems to get a real big kick out of it.

My biological father lives in Minnesota. I didn't see him until I was like about ten years old. My mother said she anguished terribly about whether I should ever meet him. At the time she even asked me what I thought. I didn't know. I was ten years old. She then decided that for my future psychological grounding, it was imperative that I bond with my biological father. So when I was almost eleven I got on this plane and went out to see him. He met me at the airport. He was real nervous. He carried this sign, but I would have known him without it. I mean he looked just like me. He took me to this little house where he lives by a stream. It's right up close to the mountains, away from everyone. It's really nice there, really nice. He like fishes and hunts and hires out on these guide jobs.

That first time, I went out for a week. Now I go for a month every summer. He's all right most of the time now too. I never told my mother or she would have have lost it, I never would have seen him again, but the first time out there he was pretty shaky. He drank a lot, and smoked dope a lot too. Not in front of me, but out by the stream. I thought it was just cigarettes at the time, but now that I've smoked it I know it was dope. He was real funny for the first couple of days, then he took like this big dive. He fought over in Vietnam, and he drank one night and talked about being over there. That was pretty strange. He became violent almost. In his eyes I mean. He would tell me stories and become real violent in his eyes, not against the people over there either, but against himself. It was like he was real mad, angry. He just wanted to explode against himself. It was pretty intense. Like I said, I was ten years old. I sat there on this chair, and he just kind of went off. For three days in a row he did that. I don't even know if he slept. When I woke up in the morning, he was either still at the kitchen table, or he walked hard back and forth across the floor, with that same angry look in his eyes. I was scared at first, I must have been. But after a while I didn't mind. In a way I was glad he told me those things, even though he seemed crazy. But it's real hard to explain. Then, after he snapped out of it, he spent the rest of the time apologizing like mad, telling me how much he loved me. So it was a pretty weird trip. I mean I was ten years old.

When I came home, my mother told me that she regretted sending me. She said she'd made the wrong decision, that the man was a certifiable lunatic. She'd been scared to death about what I might experience out there. She was surprised when I said I liked him. She even got mad I remember. I still have this feeling that she wanted me to be scared of him, to hate him, and that's why she sent me out there. It's a feeling I don't like.

He calls every couple of weeks now, just to see what's going on in my life. He even has our local paper sent way out there, just so he can read all about my basketball. He's really proud of that.

He's already like talked to the coach at the University of Minnesota too, and wants me to get a bunch of clippings together and send them out to him. And that would be really too cool if I could ever go out there to school. No shit. I mean that would be just so cool. But I know Mom would never let me though.

No more than two or three minutes after my biological father hung up, Jason called. This time, he was just about going fucking nuts. He said he was going over to the high school right then and take it out of my locker. He said he'd break the goddamn lock if he had to. I told him I'd take it out tomorrow afternoon, that one more day wasn't gonna matter none. He said he was in deep enough fucking shit at school already, and that if any other shit happened he'd be kicked out for good. I told him I'd do it tomorrow, after basketball practice. He said he'd be waiting at my locker to make sure I did. I still couldn't figure out why Jason was so upset though. It was a stupid thing to have done, I know that, but no one really knew about it at school yet, and my uncle wouldn't be back for a couple of weeks. So we had plenty of time.

My uncle's pretty different, my Uncle Tommy. But he's different from my mother I mean, not different from a lot of the people around here. He works at the paper mill, and him and my mother can't stand each other. He's got this big beer gut, huge, that sticks way out over his belt. He's proud of it too. He always tries to get me to hit it. It's as hard as a rock. He drives a pickup truck with a rifle rack, and he's got bumper stickers plastered all over saying things like, "Protected by Smith and Wesson," "Have you hugged your gun today?," "Guns equal Rights; look it up in the Constitution!," stuff like that. He's a maniac about guns. He's got hundreds of them. He says they'll all come in handy when the liberals finally take over, take away our rights, and the real revolution begins. My mother thinks he's crazy. And she hates guns. When I was growing up she never let me see my uncle. I hardly even knew he existed. I just knew there was an Uncle Tommy around town because Grammy and Grampy talked about him all the time. Then one day I was at this gas station, and the guy behind the counter happened to say his full name. When I looked, I saw this big guy standing there with this huge gut sticking out over the counter. I told him who I was. I didn't know how he'd react, but he exploded laughing and put his arm around me so hard I thought I was gonna be just about crushed against that gut of his. He took me back to his house that very day, and made me promise not to tell my mother. Then he showed me his gun collection. It covered two whole walls. He had handguns, hunting rifles, assault rifles, just about every kind of gun you could think of. He told me to come back on the sly every now and then, and he'd take me out to the range and teach me how to shoot. That way, he said, in spite of my mother, he'd see to it I didn't turn into some kind of "wine sippin', opera lovin' fairy."

Just about every Saturday afternoon then, when my mother thought I was going down to the park to play basketball, I'd bike clear over to my uncle's house. The first thing he did was to teach me all about the guns. He taught me their history, how to assemble and disassemble them, and then all the tricks on how to use them safely. He was a real stickler on that, on how to use them safely. He said the second my hand touched that gun, it was then I had to start thinking. From that point on, I had to be conscious of every move I made. No excuses either. And he wasn't kidding. I remember once I swung this rifle around without thinking, an empty rifle too, and I like crossed a part of his body with it, and shit, no joke, I thought he was gonna just about annihilate me.

Like I said, the first few times I went over we didn't even go to the range. He showed me just about every gun he had in his collection, and every single one had a story. He had one of the first Winchester repeating rifles ever made. It was used at the end of the Civil War, and then used after that to shoot buffalo. Carved into the butt were the names of four or five guys, with dates. I could've sat there for days looking at those guns and listening to his stories. Then, about the third or fourth time I went over, he chose the guns we'd work with at the range. One was a Beretta 9mm like the local police used, just so I'd know what certain people were carrying around on their hips in this town, he said. Another was a Remington .32 Special, so I'd know how to shoot a deer and feed myself when the revolution came. The last one we'd be taking out was an AK-47, a Soviet type assault rifle he called it, made in Czechoslovakia. It was first used in Vietnam, and now was the weapon of choice for drug dealers. Then he laid the ammo out and explained to me how it was made, the different types available, and which types we were going to shoot. One type, for the AK-47, was this special exploding sonic cartridge that we'd developed in Vietnam. It was real hard to get. Most countries had outlawed it. It exploded inside the object, and if it struck a part of the bone, any part, the sonic waves it gave off would like run through the rest of bone, shattering the whole thing. You could hit like a wrist, and the whole rest of the arm would be shattered. It was pretty fucking amazing.

Finally, we drove out to the range. I'd never shot a gun before, and I was pretty nervous. I was only twelve years old, so I was afraid they'd kick so hard that they'd throw me around and make me look foolish. There were different areas of the range for different guns. At handgun range, the targets were real close. At the rifle range, the targets were pretty far away. We put these plugs in our ears, then my uncle showed me how to stand, how to aim, to breathe, to squeeze. It was all stuff he'd explained hundreds of times to me back at the house. Then he passed me the Beretta. It was strange. I can't explain the feeling. The gun was not that big, not even that heavy, but I'd seen plenty of times what it can do when it hits somebody. So it was a strange feeling. I mean all that power in something so small. I aimed at the chest area. I squeezed the trigger. And I was like braced for this big kick, but there was almost nothing. A sharp pull up that settled right back, almost by itself, that's all. I fired off the whole clip. Then we reeled the target up and looked. I would've sworn every shot was like straight right into the guy's chest, but the target was clean, untouched. Only one little knick was on a shoulder. My uncle just laughed and laughed. He got a big kick out of that.

Then we moved to the rifle range. There I shot the deer rifle. And that thing just about knocked me on my ass. No joke. It just about ripped my friggin shoulder off. I told him I didn't want to do another one, but he made me stand there, brace myself, and squeeze one off. The second one kicked just as bad. My uncle could see I was scared I think. I didn't do another one.

Then my uncle got out the AK-47, the assault rifle. For a few minutes I refused to shoot. I knew it had to be a lot more power-ful than the deer rifle. My uncle kept telling me to try it, that I'd be surprised. He told me the clip held a few of those sonic bullets too. He said that I should try and hit the target, then we could see for ourselves just what kind of damage they could do. I really didn't want to shoot, but I closed my eyes, held on as tight as I could, and squeezed the trigger. I heard the crack, and I felt the gun give like this real smooth punch into my shoulder. It was amazing. I can't explain it. It was like it was greased, or sliding on a rail, really smooth. My uncle just laughed. He explained how this model had a special system of springs built into the butt to absorb the impact. I shot again, my eyes open this time. A sharp loud crack, and the same smooth punch. No joke, it was really fucking amazing. Then my uncle looked up and down the range. When he saw there was no one else in sight, he reached over and turned a little switch underneath the barrel. He looked up and down the range again, and told me that what I was about to do was illegal, that I could do it just this once, and never again. Then he told me to just squeeze the trigger once and release, as fast as I could, and to hold on. What happened next, I can't really explain either. I mean I just barely touched that trigger, just touched and released, and the gun like took off and danced. My uncle laughed, telling me I'd just squeezed off nine rounds. A tiny bit of smoke came from the barrel. I just stood there in shock almost. I never thought it could be like that, I mean the feeling. I've played video games that give you a high energy rush and stuff, that make you feel like you're ready to take on the fucking world, but when you realize what just happened in less than a second, so fast, so intense, and in real life too, I mean it was absolutely fucking awesome! I've never felt anything like it!

When we looked at the target, it was hit like only once, near a side, and the goddamn thing was blown away. No shit. Clean away. And the target was made of pretty thick straw too. In the front there was only this one perfectly round hole, but in the back, in the back the hole was blown wide open, like ten times bigger. No shit! I was real excited I remember, but my uncle got dead serious then. He pointed to the front of the target, then to the back. He put his finger in the hole and explained the damage done. Then told me never to forget that what I held in my hands was not a toy.

For a couple of summers back then, when I was thirteen and fourteen, I snuck over there on Saturday afternoons and we went out to the range. Then when I started high school I pretty much stopped going. And I used to tell Jason about it, about going to the range and all the guns my uncle had, but I could see he really never believed me. So I told him that when my uncle went away to Florida on his vacation this year, I'd take him over and show him the guns. To tell you the truth, I'd completely forgot about it, but Jason came up to me last week at school still really horny about seeing those guns. I hesitated a bit, because my uncle doesn't want anyone near his house when he's not there, no one. He's told me that over and over. But I know where he keeps a key hanging on this tree out back of his house, and I figured that as long as we left everything exactly the way we found it, there wouldn't be anything wrong with going over for a few minutes and letting Jason have a look. So last Wednesday I took him over. And he went wild when he saw those guns. Especially the AK-47, of course. I mean who wouldn't? He said how it would be great if we could show it to a couple of the guys at school. I told him no. But he kept after me, saying I could just disassemble it, slip it into school in my gym bag, show it to a couple of the guys, and then slip it back out right off. No problem. And I knew better, I did, but at the time I didn't see a big problem with it either. I mean my uncle wouldn't be home for another two weeks yet. So I broke it down, put it in my gym bag, then carried it to school. Just before basketball practice I put it in my locker. I knew it was a real stupid move, even then I did. A full clip of nineteen rounds was taped to the butt too, and I didn't even realize that until I got it to school.

I still haven't showed it to the guys yet. I'm starting to think it's not such a good idea now. And Jason, that very night we took it, he was on the phone telling me to pull it to fuck out of there, that he hadn't even thought about what was going on around the country, what with kids and guns in schools and stuff. I hadn't either. I realize now that people might be a lot more upset than I thought. But what's going on in those other schools is a lot different than this though, it's no way near the same. I mean those kids doing all of that have got to be really screwed up.

After Jason hung up, I went back to my computer and my quadratic equations. Absolute, usless shit. At some point, my mother knocked on the door. When I opened, she was out there with Gretchen. She asked me if I wanted to come down and have supper. I told her I had to study. I said that I'd grab something from the freezer later on. Then she let Gretchen come in. She even helped her up on the bed. That was a new one on me. And on Gretchen too. She just kind of looked at me, then at my mother, and then like slunk across the top of the bed. My mother turned to leave, but then sighed halfway toward the door, turned around, and came back to sit on the edge of the bed. And I knew something serious was up. The only time my mother ever comes into my room and sits on the edge of the bed, and then joins her hands, is when something serious is up. She told me she had something to tell me. She said she'd been wanting to tell me for about a week now, but was just waiting for the right time. She looked at the floor. I didn't know what it was, but I could feel my whole body go numb. Then she said Gretchen was really sick. She asked me if I remembered when she'd taken her to the vet's a couple of weeks ago. I said I did. She sighed and said it wasn't really arthritis in her hips at all, she'd just told me that because she didn't know what else to say. What Gretchen really had in her hips was cancer. Michael Jackson. I mean only a fucking idiot would stand up there grabbing his balls. And there was nothing to be done. Only some fucking idiot. And tomorrow she said, I mean only a real fucking idiot would think he's great by grabbing his fucking balls, and tomorrow she said, tomorrow she was going to have to be put to sleep.

My mother left. My dog was behind me on the bed. I couldn't study. I put her outside in the hall because I couldn't. Then I studied. She cried and scratched at the door. I studied for a long time I think. I got a lot done. I knew I had to do good on this test tomorrow. Then I played Mega-Death. I chose the most difficult setting. I used only a revolver too. People came at me from all sides, hard, furious, trying to kill me. But I remained focused. I made it all the way to Level Seven, with just a revolver. I'd never made it to Level Seven before.

I don't know when I went to bed, between twelve and one I think. I couldn't sleep. My dog still cried outside, so I couldn't sleep. I went out, picked her up, and took her down the stairs. I left her at the bottom and came back up. She still cried. But when I closed my door I couldn't hear her. And then I slept.

monday > > >

I woke up. The room was still dark. My mother called. I got up, brushed my teeth, and put on my clothes. Then I grabbed my book bag. Downstairs, breakfast was on the table again, ready. When I sat down to eat, the dog put her nose on my lap. The TV was on. "Good Morning America." Every morning, my mother drank her coffee and watched "Good Morning America." On it some huge fat guy cooked. His food was Cajun, they said, from New Orleans. I don't think my mother spoke. I didn't speak. When I was done I grabbed my book bag and left.

The morning was cold, real cold. The sun, pale white and small, real small, now broke the sky and rose above the snow. I didn't take the school bus, I walked. The cold air burned, pinched the inside of my nose. Steam left houses, cars, people's mouths, and rose white into the air. Above the snow, the sky was a deep blue. My feet crunched beneath me. Other kids walked too, small kids, but towards the Elementary School.

Jason pulled up in his car. I got in. He acted scared, nervous. He said Mike Pooler called last night and mentioned the gun. He said it meant automatic suspension, forever. I had to get it out right away, before tonight, because if Mike Pooler knew then others knew. I don't think I spoke.

At school, in the parking lot, Mike Pooler came up. He asked if it was true. If it was true he wanted to see it, but not in there, Jesus, I had to get it out of there. Why did I even bring it in there? Jason told him to shut his fucking mouth, that it was a lie, and to shut his fucking mouth.

Amanda was at the door. She asked me what was wrong. I said nothing was wrong. She said something was wrong. Jason said it was nothing, nothing. I walked down the hall towards my locker. Amanda went back and forth in front, her eyes wide, worried. She still asked what was wrong. Mike Pooler came up again, out of breath. Two cops were in the office he said, two cops were in there with Mr. Babcock. Jason pushed him, told him to get to fuck out of there. Amanda almost screamed now, her hands in fists. Jason told her to get away, to leave us alone. Then he told me to open my locker, as fast as I could, grab it and run, that he'd be out in his car.

Other kids watched, a ways away, a group of kids. Amanda still asked what was wrong. I opened my locker. My gym bag, white with its bright red cardinal, stood on end. I grabbed it, pulled it out, and went to leave. But at the far end of the corridor, Mr. Babcock and the two cops were just turning the corner. They walked fast. The cops had their hands on their hips, on their Berettas. There was no other way to leave. Mr. Babcock had an arm raised, pointed at me. The cops had their hands on their Berettas. One had flipped up the leather guard. They shouted. Their faces were hard. Groups of kids watched, frozen. I unzipped my gym bag. All was right there. Three pieces. Easy. Quick. I locked in the stock and the cannon. I snapped on the butt. I heard them holler now, loud, "Stump" and those two cops. Two kids were beside me, friends. They screamed in my ear. The AK-47 was complete in my locker, whole. The friends, a boy and a girl, screamed. I tore the clip from the butt and jammed it in. Nineteen rounds. I had nineteen rounds. I cocked back the chamber. They came at me from all sides now, all sides. I stepped back from my locker, raised, and shouldered. One cop stopped, his face white. He went for his Beretta. And that crack then. One smooth pump, that's all, like greased, or on a rail, this one smooth pump. Strange. Nothing for such a massive reaction. Nothing. The cop's chest blew, strange, in silence, you always wondered, just blew open in a deep splash of red across the screen. The other cop's Beretta was up. At 130 feet. Panicked. No time to aim. A probable miss. His round slammed into the metal of the lockers, screamed by your head. Then that crack, and that one smooth pump. The cop's thigh exploded, spinning him with the force. Babcock had turned, ran. And one of his arms went then, simply flew off. Voices screamed. They came from the left. Hard. I turned, and missed, but you have to wait till they're lined up right, just in front, and not waste, not with only one clip, nineteen rounds, and no code, no chance to pick up ammo. A girl it was, twice she was hit, strange, blown right back hard against the lockers, white upon red and red upon all the rest, her eyes locked hard. Missy. And the voices still scream. Most figures run, disappear. But some remain, dark spots, frozen, cowered against the sides, lined up against the sides down the length of the tunnel. Hard to see. Difficult. But with good breath, good stance, attainable. Some blow too when hit, pieces explode, slide along the floor. Others just slump. It's weird. And none of it violent. None of it violent at all. And then empty, like that, all nineteen rounds spent.

The bathroom was cool. Light grey on the top half, dark grey on the bottom half. The metal scraped, echoed when it hit the cement floor. The end still smoked. And very quiet here it was. Silent. The sound of water, flowing, filling. No voices. So silent. And then sirens. And then footsteps, footsteps running loud out in the hall, measured, precise. And now the voices. Screaming voices, angry voices.

part two

"I don't get it!" he said again.

He still wore his black flak jacket, was still dressed in blue. A combat knife was strapped around one calf, its blade hidden in a black plastic sheath. He stood in front of the glass wall. Behind the wall, I knew others watched. His hands were in fists. Splashes of red were still on the skin. He stepped forward and placed his fists on the table, looked straight into my face.

"I just don't get it! Two of my fellow officers are dead, do you realize that?! I mean what is going on here?! Can you tell me?! You're a basketball player for chrissakes, not a fucking assassin! You're one of the most well liked kids in your high school! Everyone knows who you are in this community! So what is going on here?! What to fuck is happening anyway?! Can you tell me that?! What?!"

His face was deep red. The veins on his neck were swollen into blue.

"Two of my fellow officers are dead! And for what?!"

My right eye still hurt. I had dried blood on my right arm, on my chest. On the glass wall I saw my reflection. My eye was swollen, almost shut. One of them had stepped on my neck, then stepped on my face, and ground his heel into my eye. Another rolled me on my back, the butt of his M-16 ready to come down hard into my ribs, when the man who looked at me now, when this man had stopped him.

Behind me, the door opened.

"Sergeant," a voice said, a calm voice, "why don't you take a break now? Go outside for a while and cool off?"

The sergeant stood and leaned back from the table. His eyes burned at me. I'd never seen eyes like that before. He turned and walked hard out of the room. The door shut. For a while things were quiet.

"Well Philip," the voice then said, "I'd say we have a lot of sorting out to do."

His steps were sharp on the floor, crisp. I heard a chair lift, then get placed on the floor in front of me, across the table. A hand touched my face, my chin, real gently. It turned my head.

"Let me take a look at that eye. I assume it's already been looked at by someone?"

I shook my head no. It hurt, but I shook my head.

"Well then I think we better get a doctor in here to see you. I don't think it's anything serious, but I think we better have a doctor look at it just to make sure." The hand released from my chin. "Someone got a little rough with you I guess, huh?"

My eyes didn't move. They still just looked at the table.

"Well, given the circumstances, I'm sure that doesn't surprise you."

He sat in the chair across from me. His hands, then his forearms, came into view. He wore a sport coat, green. The shirt cuffs were light blue.

"Now, I know you've been read your rights," he said. "I also know that you've been told you have the right to an attorney, that you needn't say a thing until an attorney is present, and that anything you do say can and will be held against you in a court of law.

There is a tape recorder running at the moment as well. You do understand all of that?"

I went to speak, but my throat was swollen and hot. Nothing moved.

"Let me get you something to drink," the man said. "What would you like, a Coke? I think we got some Snapple out there too."

I cleared my throat. The sounds I made turned, hot and thick.

"What was that?"

I tried again.

"Orange juice," I said.

"Orange juice?"

I nodded my head. It hurt awful, but I nodded. I don't know what he did. Maybe he hit a button. But the door opened.

"Would you get Philip here a big glass of orange juice, please? And why don't you make that two?"

"Well, sir," another voice said from behind, "I don't know if we . . ."

"Officer, why don't you just go get us a couple of nice big glasses of orange juice, please. I'm sure the Brewster Police Department has the means to track down some orange juice."

The door shut.

"Now, you do understand that you needn't speak to me until an attorney is present?"

I nodded.

"Does that mean you're waiving that right?"

I shrugged my shoulders.

"Philip, I'm sorry, but you must verbalize this, say it out loud. Does this mean that you're waiving your right to have an attorney present?"

"I guess so."

"I'm afraid it has to be yes, or no."

"I don't care. Yes."

"Good," the man said, "and now that we've got that out of the way, let me introduce myself. I'm Detective Ross Kimball of the State Police."

One hand slid away from its green sleeve, came across the table and stopped, almost touching my fingers. My arm hurt, but I reached for the hand and shook, as best I could.

The door opened again.

"Ah yes, here we are," the Detective said, "two big glasses of orange juice."

He had a tall paper cup, a Dairy Queen Blizzard cup, that he put it in front of me. Then he held it up off the table.

"Drink up, Philip."

I took the cup and brought it to my lips. It smelled real good, real sweet, like oranges. It was cold in my mouth, down my throat, sweet and cold. I never tasted anything so good.

"First of all, before you give me your version of what happened, tell me, where did you get access to a gun like that?"

I still drank. I drank the whole thing. I set the cup on the table.

"It's my uncle's. My Uncle Tommy's. I took it from his house."

"Well then, where did he get access to a gun like that, an AK-47 assault model? They've been banned for over two years now."

"He's had it for a long time," I said.

"It was illegally rigged to be able to shoot on automatic. Did you know that?"

I nodded.

"Did you have it on automatic?"

It hurt, but I shook my head. The detective took a drink of orange juice. He wore glasses. I didn't think he wore glasses, he didn't sound like he wore glasses, but he did. They were the round kind, with just wire along the rims. His hair was black, real black, and slicked back. He was a lot shorter than I am. Most people are, but he was a lot shorter. And he was neat. His sport-coat, his tie, his light blue shirt, everything was perfect. He didn't look like a detective. He looked like an Italian.

"Well what do you say we back up now, and let's hear from you. Yesterday, for example, could you tell me what you were doing when you . . ."

But just then the door opened, hard.

"My my," a voice said, sharp, sarcastic, "what a surprise. Having a little private one-on-one chat, are we?"

I looked up. I recognized him. He was a friend of Sidney's. Jack. A lawyer. I'd seen him just two days before at Sidney's funeral. Him and Sidney had grown up together in New York. He always came up twice a year, and they went fishing. Jack was pretty famous too. He was always on TV, talking about trials on talk shows, on the news.

"Ah yes, Counselor Shapiro, we got your message. We've been waiting for you."

"Oh, I'm sure you have."

"And your client here waived his right to have an attorney present for the time being, and so I . . ."

"Now, why doesn't that surprise me?" Jack said, his voice still sarcastic; "a seventeen-year-old who, completely cognizant of the law, of course, and after carefully weighing all possible consequences, waives his right to an attorney. It seems to me I've run into this situation innumerable times before, and that judges somehow always seem to have a hard time buying your side of it. And yet, here we are again."

The detective just sort of smiled. He shrugged his shoulders.

"Well I happen to be his lawyer, so you can consider his right reinstated," Jack said. "Unless, of course, you want to officially interrogate my client right now, right at this moment, in your obvious state of chaos. He'll have nothing to say, and I'm sure the Prosecution will love you for your haste. At least I know the Defense will."

The Detective sort of smiled again.

"Oh that's all right, Counselor. Now that you're here, I suppose we can hang around the usual number of weeks waiting for you to decide to cooperate."

He pushed out from the table and stood. He held up his container of orange juice.

"Orange juice, Counselor?" he said.

"No thanks. I think I'll pass."

"Well, you can confer with your client in here if you like, I'll be right outside should you want me."

"Hardly, Detective," Jack said. He nodded towards the glass wall. "This is not my first time round the barn. Conferring in a miked room with a gallery of police looking on hardly qualifies as private. There must be a retaining cell empty somewhere. A simple retaining cell will do just fine."

"As you like. I'm sure we can find you something. I'll send an officer right in."

The detective left. Jack put an arm on my shoulder and bent down close.

"I was on my way to court this morning when your mother called me, Philip. I dropped everything and flew right up. That's a bad-looking eye, did they do that to you?"

I nodded.

"Did you resist arrest? The arrest report said you didn't."

"I don't think so. No."

"And they did that to you? Well, we'll definitely have some pictures taken of that." He moved in a little closer. "How long have you been talking with the police? I mean in here like this?"

"Just a couple of minutes."

"I'll hear it all on tape later, but for now, just so I'll know, what did he ask you about?"

"About the gun, where I got it."

"You told him?"

I nodded.

"Anything else?"

"No. I don't think so."

"Good."

The door opened again. Jack helped me to stand. My legs were like rubber, real weak. My arms and chest were sore. My head throbbed awful. Jack was looking at me.

"You could probably use some aspirin, couldn't you Philip?"

I nodded again. Jack held me by an arm and we walked out the door.

"Just a second," the police officer said. He turned me around, pulled my arms back, and put on handcuffs like before. Like before too they felt strange. They were tight on my wrists. My fingers touched flat together.

"Okay, go ahead."

"Behind the back?" Jack said. "Is that necessary?"

"Behind," the officer said.

Out in the office, everything went quiet. People stopped and looked at me. I heard the voices of two women cry, not an angry cry, but sad. A man in a white shirt and tie shook his head, looked away. The officer led us past them and through a metal door. Beyond the metal door was a long grey corridor lit only by lights. It was quiet, real quiet. Halfway down, the cells began, on the right and on the left. At the very end, the officer took a key from his belt and opened a metal bar door. The sound of metal, of the key in the lock, of the door that slid open, they echoed loud in the quiet. Inside the cell, a grey bench lined one wall.

"Thank you, Officer," Jack said. "And yes, could you take his cuffs off, please?"

The officer stepped behind me. Pressure released on my wrists. My arms pulled to the front, by themselves, and my breath released too, breathed in real deep. I don't know why.

"I'll be right outside," the officer said, and he slid the cell door shut. He locked it.

Jack pulled the grey bench away from the wall.

"Have a seat, Philip," he said.

Bars rose on two of the sides, all the way to the ceiling.

Jack sat down beside me. He took a deep breath and looked down between his legs. He shook his head. His hair hung towards the floor.

"Jesus," he said. "I certainly never expected to be here in this situation. And certainly not with you." He stayed like that, with his head hung there, then breathed again and straightened up.

"Well, regardless of my amazement," he said, "we'd better get started. I'd like to get you out there quickly and favorably surprise them. Favorable surprises do have a way of keeping them off balance. And that detective you were with, I've seen my fair share, and I can spot a cagey one when I see one. We're going to have to be alert." He crossed his legs. He had on black shiny loafers with tiny tassels. His stockings were black, and so thin you could see through to the skin. "Now, after they've interrogated for a while, they'll probably bring in something to eat and sit back and make a few jokes, try to be real cool, but we will not take our eye off the ball, will we Philip? Remember, you don't have to say a word in there. You don't even have to give your name. When they ask a question, let me do the talking. If I feel you should answer, I will turn to you and instruct you to do so directly. Is that clear? I know I'm asking you to take in a lot in a very short time, but these first few hours are always the most crucial in any case. So is all this clear?" He reached over and patted my thigh. "It's going to be a long day, Philip. It will run late into the night. The more tired people are the more maneuverable they will become, it's an ancient method, and they still use it. But I'll be beside you all the while. And you do understand me now, don't you? I know you've gone through hell and are not thinking clearly, but do you understand every word I'm saying?"

"Yes," I said.

"Are you sure?"

I nodded.

"Okay. Let's get down to business then, and the first thing I want you to remember, to keep clear in your mind, is that you do not realize what you did."

I looked up. He was leaned forward again, his elbows on his knees.

"But I do. I mean I can go through every single . . ."

"Philip. Listen to me. You don't realize what you did. How could you? If you realized, you wouldn't have done it. Therefore, you don't realize what you did."

"But I do, I mean I . . ."

"Philip, trust me on this, you don't. And when and if they ask you that particular question, and I instruct you to respond, that's what you say; 'I don't realize what I did.' And that's all you're going to say in there. So say it for me. C'mon, I want to hear you say it."

"Right now?"

"Yes."

"But why?"

"Just say it. It's important."

My eye still hurt awful.

"What about the aspirin? You said you were going to . . ."

"Philip, for chrissakes, just say it. We don't have much time.

These first few hours are the most important. And it must appear as if we're being entirely open. You'll have the aspirin shortly."

Each of the words crawled into my mind by itself, real slow.

"I don't, I don't realize what I did."

"Good. Now say it again. And say it like you really mean it this time, slowly, with sadness and a sense of amazement in your voice. And don't be afraid to shake your head slowly if it helps. Like this." He was slowly shaking his head, looking at the floor. "'I just don't realize what I did.' So go ahead, say it again."

I shook my head. It hurt, but I shook my head.

"I just don't realize what I did."

"Better. Much better. Now keep going over that in your head. And remember, it's the truth. You'll only be telling them the truth." He reached into his shirt pocket and pulled out a package of gum. He peeled the wrapper off a stick and handed it to me. "A piece of gum?"

I took it. He peeled the wrapper off another piece, put in his mouth, and began to chew. I put mine in my mouth, tried to chew, but it hurt too much. So I just let it sit there. It made this pool of spit that I could swallow, sweet with the juice of the gum. It felt good down my throat.

"Now, first point: During their questioning you say nothing unless I instruct you to, and I will only do that once, maybe twice, during our whole time in there, and each time you will say, 'I don't realize what I did.' Second point: whatever you do, don't let their emotion get to you. Just shut up. Don't blab out anything. And most of all, and Jesus, listen to me now Philip, most of all, don't give any reasons for having done it. Whatever reasons you think you may have are the wrong ones anyway, and they'll just jump on them to establish premeditation and motivation. In other words, 'I don't realize what I did' is the only thing you're going to say. Do you understand all of this, Philip?"

I nodded.

"What did I say then?"

"To just shut up," I said. "Except for that one thing, to just shut up."

"Good boy. I wish we had time to run through this better, but we don't. It's necessary that they see us as cooperating as quickly and as best we can, that may make them be a little less thorough. The media's already flooding this place, and the police are out there chomping at the bit, that I can tell you. But I'll be with you all the time. Remember, just keep your mouth shut until I instruct you to open it, and then the one sentence. And I can't seem like I'm coaching you either. If you start some kind of other answer, you're on your own. It's illegal for me to coach your answers. That's why you have to keep quiet. In the state you're in, anything you have to say can only harm us. Do you understand?"

I nodded. He put his arm round me. He had on cologne. I didn't smell it before, but he had on cologne that smelled like spice.

"And I know at the moment that you don't care about any of this, that you know you're guilty and you just want the worst to be done to you, but your opinion will soon change on that, believe me."

He kept his arm round me and chewed his gum for a while. I didn't feel like he said either, not at all. The cell was real quiet. Overhead were two lights in metal cages. Then he told me I would most likely be put on a suicide watch, that I would be in a cell monitored by a camera for a few days, for my own safety. He agreed with that call, he said. Then he said his partner would fly up very early in the morning, before the arraignment, Danny Ryan. Then he talked about what was going to happen, the procedure. I would be arraigned before a judge some time tomorrow, and the charges would be formally made. Then the team would have some time to ourselves, that's what he called us now, a team, to study the prosecution's likely approach, and to begin to formulate a strategy. Then he sat there quiet for a minute again. He took a deep breath, and his body just let go. He spoke of my mother, of how I wouldn't see her until after the questioning. And then he asked me if I'd been real close to Sidney, if I'd been bothered by Sidney's passing away so unexpectedly. I went to say no, but before I could, he suddenly said to ignore that question, to act like he never even said it, that, if need be, we could bring up the usefulness, the pros and cons of such a feeling when we conferred as a team.

"Now," he said, and he stood, "let's shock the old hell out of 'em and say we're ready to go."

He called down the corridor. Footsteps echoed loud outside the cell. The officer turned the corner. Jack said we were ready to go. The officer looked surprised. He unlocked, and then slid the bar door open.

At the door, he motioned for me to turn around. I turned, put my hands behind my back, and he put on the handcuffs. Then we walked back down the long grey corridor. When he pushed opened the metal door, everyone out there looked up and went silent again. And lots of people were out there too. They stood like statues, posters, all real still. Then farther off I heard running, shouting. A woman came up to a rail. She was held back by two cops. Her face was twisted, all twisted in hate. She screamed.

"You're a monster!" she said. She leaned out hard over the rail, her face all twisted. "You're nothing but a fucking monster!"

A man was behind her. He had his hands on her shoulders and pulled. He didn't scream, he just looked sad. It was Missy's father. The man was Missy's father. The woman had to be Missy's mother. I didn't recognize her, I still didn't, but that's who it had to be. I've known her ever since I was little, ever since Missy and me have been friends. I used to go over to their house all the time. But I still didn't recognize her. A man in a suit came up and hurried us along.

"For chrissakes, Humphries," he said, "don't you know enough to bring him in through the back way? From now on, bring him in through the back!"

We went into the same room as before, the one with the long glass wall. The first detective, the one who looked like an Italian, Detective Kimball, was in there with another guy, a fat guy. They both were standing. Detective Kimball pointed to a chair. Jack told them I didn't really have anything to say at the moment. They said they just wanted to talk to me in general, try to clear a few things up. Jack sat beside me in the chair. A big glass of orange juice was right in front of me.

"Drink up, Philip," Detective Kimball said, with a nice smile.

I picked up the cup and drank the whole thing in a couple of gulps. Then they asked questions, questions about the school, about my morning, about how long I had the gun in the school, but Jack just said I wasn't going to answer. I thought they'd get mad at that, frustrated, but they didn't. They never looked at Jack either, they looked straight at me, asked only me the questions. I wanted to answer, I mean they were simple questions that I knew the answers to. And the detectives were nice, they didn't act upset at all, but I just kept my mouth shut like Jack had said. Then, at some point, a long time later, Jack told them that I didn't realize what I'd done.

"Is that right, Philip?" the other detective said.

Jack nodded, and told me to answer the question. I looked down at the table. I shook my head like Jack had showed me.

"I don't realize what I did," I said.

Under the table, Jack patted me on the knee. Then they asked different kinds of questions, questions that weren't questions. They asked me why I had such anger in me, where it came from, but I'd never told them I had anger in me. I wanted to answer. Jack knew it too. Under the table, his hand squeezed my thigh. But I wanted to answer. I wasn't angry. I never get angry. I've never even felt anger in my life, I don't think. But Jack got up quick from the table. He said that was enough, that I had no more to say, that I needed my sleep.

"Look, Counselor," Detective Kimball said, "if the kid wants to answer that question, just let him answer it."

Jack looked at his watch.

"It's two-thirty in the morning, Detective, and we have nothing more to say. We didn't even have to come in here to begin with, so what do you say you let the young man get some sleep? He's going to have a full day tomorrow."

The officer came in and put the handcuffs back on. Outside, the office was still full of people, even at that time of the morning. Jack said we were going to see my mother. All day, I hadn't even thought of my mother. Not once, I don't think. The officer took us to a glassed in office across the way. We walked by people that still stopped and stared, even at that time of the morning. I saw the back of my mother's head through the glass. She sat at a desk, alone. She turned and looked at me as I came. I didn't recognize her face either. I knew it was my mother's, but the eyes weren't the same. They were red, full of tears, but it's not the color or the tears I mean, they just weren't the same. They were wide open, deep. They were big black holes. I don't know how else to put it. They took me in, they surrounded me, all weak and crying and coming from my mother, taking me all the way in, like I'd never felt them before, but it was just too late, I don't know how else to put it. She ran to me and held me. My hands were cuffed behind my back. I felt her tears, this wet on my face. I wanted her to stop crying. She didn't have to cry. There was no reason to cry. It just made people feel uncomfortable.

I sat beside her. She had a handkerchief in her hands. She pulled at it and pulled at it. She tried to speak, I think. She'd say my name, then begin, but all she did was cry. Jack stood beside her, with an arm around her shoulders. I'd never seen my mother like that. I've never seen anyone like that. I felt bad for her. It was hard to see.

After a few minutes, Jack told her she could see me again tomorrow, before the arraignment. Then he led her out of the office. I sat there, me and the two officers that stood beside me, until Jack returned. He said he was leaving now, going to find a hotel, and not to talk to a soul about anything the rest of the night.

"Yes, and no," he said. "That's all I want you to say. Clear?"

I nodded. Then the two officers took me into a long bathroom. They told me if I had to go I'd better go now. I said I did. They changed my handcuffs around to the front. I sat on a toilet bowl, and an officer stood in front of me. There was no door either, he just stood there. Then he asked me if I was done. I said yes, and he undid my handcuffs so I could wipe myself. He flushed the toilet, told me to stand, then cuffed me behind my back again. We walked out and into another room with wooden shelves. It looked like a locker room, an equipment room. There they undid my handcuffs and told me to strip naked. The floor was cold, concrete. Then one officer told me to bend over. He put on white gloves. He scooched down and looked up into my asshole I think. He spread it apart, and told me to cough. I coughed. He put a finger up there and felt around. It really hurt. When that was over he made me open my mouth. He pulled my lips apart and looked everywhere inside. Then the other officer handed me a pair of orange slippers and a uniform. When I took it, the uniform, it felt real light. I'd never felt anything so light. Then, when

I put it on, I saw that it was made of paper, these overalls, all made of blue paper. I'd never worn anything made of paper before either. Suicide watch. That came into my mind then, what Jack had said, for a few days, for my own safety.

We walked down a hallway and then up a staircase. At the top was another hallway lined with doors, solid doors. An officer unlocked one, and then stepped aside so I could go in. The inside was empty. I'd never seen a room so empty. There were no windows. The floor was grey, and the walls and the ceiling were all white. A small bed was against one wall. There was nothing on it either, no covers I mean. A pot with a handle was beside the bed. One of the officers told me that blankets were not allowed in here, but that the room would be kept comfortable. High up in the corners, over by the door, and then opposite the door, there were two cameras.

The two officers left. They didn't say anything, they just left. The door was white like the walls and you could hardly see it, just the lines of a rectangle a little if you looked. There was no doorknob either. And I didn't hear any music. That was weird. I expected to hear music. In most rooms where I've been that look like that, in elevators, at the dentist's, even at the vet's, there's music. But here there was nothing. I sat on the mattress. A small pillow was up at one end. It was made of paper too. Then the lights dimmed. They went from white to this dim orange almost. Up in the corners I saw the cameras move, turn real slow towards the bed. Suicide watch. I've never understood that. Why any one would want to I mean. There was this kid at school I knew, or at least sort of knew, and he committed suicide a couple of years ago. I just could never understand it.

I laid back on the bed. I closed my eyes. I wanted to sleep. More than anything I wanted to sleep. But it was so quiet. I heard my own breathing, my own heart. I could even feel my blood pump, no joke, feel it like pump out into my veins. If I was home I'd put on a CD, the TV, anything. It was just too quiet. I opened my eyes. A monster. I didn't feel like a monster. I got up from bed. I walked in that strange orange light. I heard the cameras whir as they turned, following me when I walked. I didn't feel like a monster. I didn't feel any different. I didn't know if this made me a criminal either. Gretchen had to be dead by now. She had to be. I didn't want to be a criminal.

I laid down on the bed again. I closed my eyes. I really wanted to sleep. Not so I could wake up from a bad dream because I knew it wasn't a dream. I mean, Gretchen had to be dead by now. But I couldn't sleep, and I don't know why. I've never slept without covers before though. It's hard. That was most of it I think. Even when it's hot I pull like a sheet up over me, just to have something around me, to get down inside of. But here I just laid on the top, out in the open. I curled up tight all night, trying to sleep. And that's the worst feeling I've ever had, exposed like that, uncovered. They watched me up there too. Someone watched me, and I couldn't get away, I couldn't hide my body.

The lights came up. They went quick from that strange dark orange and into this bright white. The door opened in from the wall, and a police officer stood there. I got up out of bed. And I didn't know when it was. That was strange. With no windows you can't know when it is. I don't think I slept either, but a lot of times you think that only to wake up and realize you did. But with no windows your eyes can't open, can't notice the change. He motioned for me to come forward.

"Your breakfast will be served down there," he said, "from that window. Go get it and come back here."

I looked down to the end of the corridor, but I couldn't see a window. I walked down, and when I got there this wooden panel slid open. A hand passed a tray through an opening, and the panel slid shut. On the tray was a paper cup full of milk, two pieces of toast, a lump of butter, a little paper container of jam, and a plastic spoon.

I picked up the tray and walked back to my room. I sat on the bed. The officer stayed up there in the doorway. I drank my milk. It was warm. I hate warm milk, but it still tasted good. And the toast was cold. All I had to spread the butter on with was a spoon. I'd never tried to spread butter with a spoon before. It's not all that easy. At least not hard butter on cold toast. I mean I like ripped it to shreds. But I was starved. And the jam was straw-berry, my favorite.

When I was done, the officer told me to walk back down the corridor and leave the tray by the window. Then he put handcuffs on me, and led me down to the same long bathroom as the night before. He watched me as I sat on the toilet, took my handcuffs off so I could wipe myself, and then led me out into the equip-ment room. A new set of clothes was in there for me. My own clothes. My favorite sweater, and these pants that my mother calls slacks and that I hate.

Another officer came in. They cuffed my hands behind my back like the day before and we walked out into the office. It was full of people, real noisy and full of people. When I walked in they all stopped again. They all went quiet and looked. A bright flash went off, and I saw two policemen holler and rip a camera from some guy's hands. A big clock on the wall said twenty minutes after seven. A ways away, light came up some stairs and in through a door window, daylight, and I knew it wasn't night. It was pretty early, only twenty minutes after I usually get up, and the place was still full of people.

The two policemen led me through a door and into another office, one I hadn't seen before. They unlocked my handcuffs. Jack was in there with another guy. They both held out their hands and had these real friendly smiles on their face. The other guy had bright red hair. Jack said he was his partner, Danny Ryan. He was dressed real sharp too, in this shiny dark blue suit and this flowered tie, and he spoke strong like he came from New York City. The minute I sat down, Jack handed me a big bag of Dunkin Donut muffins and a half gallon of ice cold milk. I told him I was starved. Jack just said that somehow he wasn't surprised.

Jack waited until I'd wolfed down three of those muffins, then him and his partner pulled up a chair. The room became real quiet, serious.

"Philip," Jack said, "it's time we got down to business." He had a little paper book in his hand. "First of all, this here is a manual of the legal terms used during a criminal trial. I want you to read it carefully and know them all by heart. When they come up, we're not going to have the time to stop and explain them to you." He laid the book in front of me, and then put a hand on my arm. "Now, Philip, we're going to talk honestly here, openly. I involve my clients in everything that goes on. I'm going to say things that may distress you, but these are realities we're going to be dealing with every day, and you will have to learn to approach them matter of factly, just like another day at the office. And the first thing is the predicament you find yourself in." He left his hand on my arm. "You'll be tried as an adult, and the death penalty can be sought in this state if two or more homicides have been committed during the perpetration of a felony; that is, a felony such as aggravated assault with a deadly weapon. And, being given the present climate in this country, there is no doubt in our minds that the state, the prosecution, is going to seek the death penalty in this case." Jack pulled his arm away. And I don't know what I felt then. It didn't surprise me, the words I mean, but I don't know what I felt. "Now, Danny and I have literally been up all night looking at this situation from every possible angle, trying to figure out the best way to proceed. We came up with only two plausible scenarios. The first is to go to trial and try to have you declared innocent by reason of temporary mental incompetence. Being given your relatively stable history, your status in the community, that could prove a difficult task. We would have to show your action to have been caused by what is termed 'a delusional state totally beyond rational control,' and if we weren't successful in doing that, the results could be disastrous. If the jury didn't buy it, for example, and found you guilty, it would be a much smaller step for them to then sentence you harshly, since they would have already gone through all the anxiety inherent in a case like this, already come to a sense of justification in their own minds. Do you follow me, Philip? Please stop me if you don't understand the least little thing."

"No," I said. "I think I understand."

"Good. Now this state, when dealing with capital crimes such as homicide, has what is called a bifurcated judiciary system. That is, there can be two separate trials; one for the conviction or non-conviction, and the other for the sentencing. Two entirely separate trials. You'll read about it in your manual. Do you generally understand what I mean?" I nodded. "Good. Now, here is what Danny and I have come up with. Since there is no real question of your guilt in this matter, I mean basically an entire school witnessed the act, we think it would be to our benefit to plead guilty, and then to proceed with a jury trial for the sentencing. We think the jurors would tend to see things in a different light then. They will not be the ones to have found you guilty, they will not feel themselves personally responsible for their judgment, and they will not have rid themselves of all their emotion yet, either. After all the initial anger and disbelief have died down, and when it's only you they're concentrating on, only you they're seeing every day, we feel their emotion will turn in our favor. Or at least that's our thought. We really do believe that they will be more inclined to see you in an empathetic, compassionate light. Any questions so far?" I shook my head. Jack put an arm around my shoulder and leaned in closer. He still smelled like spice. "So you see Philip, this is serious business. This is a battle for your life we're talking about here. That's why I'm going to be an absolute bastard when we're together, so expect it. In here we spill out everything. No truth is too hard or too harsh. And Danny and I will do anything, dig up anything, cast a bad light upon anyone, even people close to you, to save your life. You'll have to be ready for that." He leaned away from me then. He pointed towards the wall. "Out there," he said, "I'm an actor. But in here, I'm a realist. In here we spill our guts, lay it all out on the table. Then I package it, and I go out there and present it as favorably as I possibly can. And as for the real truth as to why you did this, that's not what we're looking for right now. And what's more, at least at this juncture, Danny and I don't care. We're here for two reasons, and two reasons only; number one is to save your life, and number two is to get you the lightest sentence possible." Jack pulled away and ran his fingers through his hair. He took a deep breath. And for the first time then I realized he was pretty tired. "So Philip, at the arraignment, we're gonna shock the old ass right off 'em and plead guilty. Just like that. And you'll see some goddamn scrambling around the DA's office then. Our goal is, of course, to always keep one step ahead of them. That's the name of the game. And by proceeding in the way I've stated, by pleading guilty and then going on to a jury trial for sentencing, Danny and I both like the way this whole thing begins to feel. But the very best we can hope for, you know, is fifteen to twenty years without possibility of parole. That's the very best we can hope for."

"Fifteen to twenty years?" I said. And I don't know why. I didn't know what they meant, and I didn't care, they were just numbers.

Jack made sure he turned up under a bit, made sure he looked straight into my eyes.

"Philip," he said, "you'll be a very fortunate human being if we can get you that. And if we can, you'll be able to leave still a relatively young man."

Jack pulled away and stood. Danny Ryan spoke then. I had a hard time paying attention, listening. He mentioned some kind of preliminary psychiatric evaluation right after, then seeing my mother, then the arraignment, but I was on the basketball court I think, going through these plays I've made on the basketball court, reliving them I guess. That happens sometimes. That's happened before when a lot of things are going on too fast around me. I can't stop it sometimes.

Jack knocked on the door and the officer came in. He put the cuffs on me again, and outside people still jostled and hollered. I didn't look up. I didn't want to any more. We crossed the main office to another room with no windows. A man was in there with a beard, sitting in an armchair. He got up to shake my hand, but had to wait until the handcuffs were unlocked. That made him look awkward, and I don't think he liked to look awkward. He introduced himself, Doctor something. He made me sit on a stool, and for a long time he looked into my eyes with a little pen light. A long time. Then he asked me simple questions, like my name, my age, my date of birth, things like that. Then he sat in his armchair, I sat on my stool, and we talked. He asked me questions mostly about school, and about playing basketball, so I had no trouble answering. At times he seemed surprised too that I answered them so easily, but I like to talk about basketball, I always have, there was no reason for him to be surprised.

The officer came in and put the cuffs on again. This time we walked down a corridor I'd never seen yet. At the end was a big glassed-in room full of sunlight. When we walked in, the light came in strong off the snow outside and hurt my eyes. I could hardly see. But the room was full of tables, tables with like panes of glass across the middle. People were in there at two of the tables. A man in blue was at each one, and someone else sat across from him. Other officers made them all get up and leave when I came in. I don't know why, but up until then I'd thought I was in there alone. I'd never thought of it as a jail, that I was in there with men who were in a jail.

The officer took off my cuffs, and I sat at one of the tables. Then he stood against the wall, only a few feet away. The sun came in bright. The floor was made of shiny wooden squares. The light reflected pretty and warm off all that deep brown. Then the door opened and my mother came in. She didn't look up. The officer stepped away from the wall and pulled out a chair. She sat, put her hands on the table, and still didn't look up. She was shaking. I'd never seen my mother shake before either.

"Hi Mom," I said.

She was close to crying. She took a deep breath, then put a hand to her mouth, pressed it hard, and looked off to the side.

"I just got done talking to Jack," I said. "He was telling me things don't look too bad."

"Oh, Philip," was all she said. She shook her head, her hands pressed tight now against her eyes, then her forehead.

"But I was just talking to him," I said. "And he's got this plan. He says like in maybe only fifteen years I can get out. I added it up, and that makes like thirty-two years old. That ain't that bad."

"Oh, Philip," she said again, but this time she ripped her hands fast away from her face. Her eyes were like two big cuts, two deep slashes, all red, raw. "Don't you realize what you did?!"

"Yes," I said, "but that's what Jack was just telling me. Honest. You can go ask him if you want."

She cried then. She tried to stop herself two or three times, and almost did. It was hard to see, to understand. I didn't like it, didn't like the way I felt I mean, real cold inside, like I didn't care.

"There's no reason to cry, Mom," I think I said, even though I didn't want to say it, didn't even care.

But she left then. She put a hand over her mouth and just left, ran towards the door. The officer stood there and watched her. I told him my mother was never like that, never. I hoped he would, but he didn't say anything.

I thought I'd have to get up then, and move to still another room, but the officer told me to sit right there. Then, a few minutes later, a man dressed in white came in carrying a tray. On it was a glass of milk, french fries, ketchup, and real Kentucky Fried Chicken. I was starved. When I was finished, the officer pointed at me and told me not to move, to just sit there. I didn't understand really. I just needed to stand for a minute. I never sit for too long. So I went to stand and he came over, grabbed me by a shoulder, and practically drove me down in the chair. Real hard.

"You sit in that goddamn chair and don't you move," he said. "You're mine now, and don't you forget it. If you move again, you'll pay."

I didn't understand. He had no right to be like that. I hadn't done anything to him. No one had a right to be like that. I was going to tell Jack. I knew Jack would do something about it.

The man in white came in and picked up the tray. For a long time I sat at the table and didn't move. It was ridiculous. It made no sense. I wasn't used to doing nothing. The officer stood against the wall, his hands behind his back. The room had twelve tables, four rows of three, each table with a chair at each end. If full, it would sit twenty-four. I was at the second table on the first row, near the side door, away from the windows. The floor was like the one at Boston Garden too, I realized that at some point. It was just like the one the Celtics played on, a parquet floor. I'd always wanted to be a Celtic. I still did. But I knew I was going to have to be a point guard in college because of my size, even though I was a power forward in high school. That's why I work on my ball handling all the time. I would've loved to try and dribble a basketball on the parquet floor in that room too, instead of just sitting there doing nothing, but I didn't ask. I didn't think there was much chance of the guy getting me one.

A long time later, Jack and Danny came in. They were both

dressed real sharp, carrying briefcases. The officer cuffed my hands in the front this time, and when we left the room he walked a ways behind us. Real low, I told Jack what he'd been like to me. Jack just kind of tightened his lips. He took a quick breath in, and said, "This ain't no country club, Philip." And that's all he said. He stopped right there. I didn't expect that either. I thought he'd be on my side. I didn't expect that.

We walked back through the main office. If anything, even more people were jammed in there. It was hot now too, close. Some guys had cameras around their necks. Others watched us go by and wrote like crazy on these paper pads. Some shouted questions too, but I couldn't make them out. Three more police officers joined us, kind of like surrounded us. We headed out onto this long glassed-in ramp that led to the next building, a big brick building I knew was the courthouse. Down below, out on the street, a big crowd of people looked up. They pointed. People with TV cameras were down there too, and everyone was pointing, shouting, beginning to run towards the courthouse. All around, the sun came in through the glass, bright off the new snow, blinding me. We walked along the ramp. It sloped up and was covered with a red rug. On each side the rug wasn't wide enough, and out there the ramp was made of this real rough concrete. At the top we entered this huge lobby, dark, all done in wood. Towards the front of the courthouse, a rope was across the big marble steps and people came barreling in past the doors, shouting questions, flashing cameras. Jack told me to look straight ahead, not to acknowledge them. Him and Danny pulled a bit ahead, walking towards the courtroom door. The officers came in real close to me. I felt an elbow.

"You're famous now, kid," one of them said in my ear. "I guess you got your goddamn wish."

The big wooden doors to the courtroom opened. We moved

inside. And suddenly it was real quiet, quiet and cool. The voices
and the shouting seemed far away. I'd never been in a courtroom
before. I'd only seen them on TV, especially the one during the
O.J. trial. My mother had that thing on every day, and it looked
pretty much like that. It was all done in wood. Rows of benches
led down to where a judge sat up there where he's supposed to sit.
The plaque in front of him said Judge McLaughlin. He was older,
but had red hair almost like Danny's. Jack and Danny walked
with me down the aisle, and we sat in front at the table on the left.
Two men and a woman were already at the table on the right.

The Prosecution, the other guys on the right, they spoke first.
They read the charges and then, like Jack said, the woman that
spoke said that the state would be seeking the death penalty, Your
Honor, death by lethal injection. Then she started talking about
how the country had had enough, but the judge came down real
hard with his gavel then. He told her to save it for the trial, that
this wasn't the time and she knew it. Nor was it the time to throw
around emotional terms like death by lethal injection either, he
said, and so she'd better stop the damn grandstanding right then
and there, for if that was the foot she wanted to start out on then
she'd better find someone else to replace her, because he'd stand
for none of that sophomoric crap in his courtroom. She turned
pretty white then, and just kind of mumbled, "I'm sorry Your
Honor."

Jack stood. He didn't say much at all, but he spoke real smooth.
Then at the end he said there was no sense in wasting the state's
time or money, and so to expedite matters, we'd be entering a
plea of guilty on all charges. And no shit, when he said that, the
guys over there on the right just about had a fit. Their heads
whipped over this way, and their eyes were bugged right out. The
woman stood, exploded off her chair. She started almost screaming that if that wasn't grandstanding on our part, then what was

it?! This was hardly the time for that either, she said, and the judge just gaveled her down again, saying that if the defense wanted to enter a plea at midnight, why then, as far as he was concerned, they were more than welcome to do it. And that was it. Six minutes it took, that's what the papers said afterwards, the whole arraignment took only six minutes.

It was harder to get out of the courtroom, to go back to the police station, than it was to get in. A whole ring of police were out there now, trying to keep the people back. When we got to the station the other officers left, and mine took me into the equipment room. There he told me to strip. I asked to keep my book, my manual that Jack had given me. He looked at it real close, flipped through all the pages, asked me for sure if my lawyer had given it to me, and handed it over even though it killed him to. Then I got dressed in blue paper again. Then he took me up the stairway to that room with white walls, a white ceiling, and no windows.

I had nothing to do. It was still the middle of the afternoon. I couldn't very well go to sleep. I couldn't figure out why they would put me there in the middle of the afternoon, with nothing to do, dressed in blue paper. I thought it had to be a mistake. I knocked on the door, but no one came. I looked up at the camera and pointed. Still nothing happened. Then I knocked hard on the door again. This time it opened, fast. The officer, "my" officer, stood there. He had one hand on his Beretta, around the handle, the leather guardstrap undone, ready to draw. With the other hand he pointed, drove his finger hard into my chest.

"Listen Mister," he said, his eyes as hard as his voice, scary, "you sit in this goddamn cell and you shut up. If I hear one more fucking word from you, I'll put you in a place that'll make this room feel like heaven."

He shut the door. I thought there had to be a mistake. The way he talked to me, he made a mistake. I wasn't like that. He didn't have to talk to me like that. And all I wanted was something to do. Like just give me a basketball. If I could've just had a basketball to hold. I mean I know it sounds stupid, but if I could like just have a basketball, a cheap one, I didn't care, one of those outdoor rubber things. It didn't matter. But why did they want me to sit here with nothing to do?

I laid on the bed. I could feel my heart pound real fast. Maybe the thought came to me then that I was in jail, I don't know. It didn't feel like a jail. It didn't look like any of the jails I'd ever seen. I closed my eyes and tried to calm down, to stop my heart from beating like that. It was real hard. I felt so scared, like this pure bright white was screaming inside, that's the only way I can explain it. But there was nothing in front of me to make me scared, so I didn't know why. I got out my manual. I looked at the words, and they were just like not even there. I made my lips move as I tried to read, but they still weren't real. I've never felt that before. It's like they were way outside and nothing could penetrate, nothing. Then on page three I saw a word I recognized. Bifurcation. I read the meaning after it, and I'd never read anything like I read those words either, so close, so intense, like I was holding on to every single letter. It was like Jack had said too, two separate trials, one to find a verdict, the other for sentencing. And that helped a bit I think, reading something I understood, that made me think of Jack and Danny. Then I thought of another word, and went back in the manual and found "arraignment." And the judge had been right, an arraignment was just for the filing of charges, nothing more. Then I began to read all the rest of the terms. And it was strange. It was probably the most boring book I'd ever had to read in my life, but I couldn't read it fast enough. For a while the room like disappeared. I was about halfway through when the door opened. The officer waved to me to get off the bed. It was suppertime, he said. He pointed down to the end of the corridor. I walked down, the wooden door slid open, a tray slid out, pushed by a hand. I grabbed it and walked back to the room. I sat on the bed and ate. The officer stood just inside the door and looked at the wall. There was mashed potato, these burnt kind of fish sticks, ketchup, and mushy green beans, all lukewarm. I still only had a plastic spoon, kind of hard to get through those fish sticks with, but I was starved. After I finished, the officer picked up the tray, shut the door, and I began to read my manual again.

When the light turned from white down into that dim orange, I was almost on the last page. I didn't know what time it was. I couldn't know. I don't know if that bothered me or not. I don't think so though. I knew that I'd close my eyes, try to sleep, and then at some time another day would begin. The only difference was they'd have to tell me when it did. They could start it any time they wanted to, or not start it at all. They could keep me there, feed me food, I'd see no daylight, and never know. But that was my imagination. I knew in real life they wouldn't. But I realized that's what I had to do now too, kill my imagination. With them in control there was no room for imagination. It would only make things worse. I was dressed in blue paper. I was in an all white room with no windows. It was their imagination I was in.

I closed my eyes. I tried to sleep. But I still just laid there out in the open, without any covers. That's real hard to get used to. I didn't know when I was going to realize I was in jail either. Part of me did already, a small part, but I didn't know what I'd be like inside when the rest of me did. I didn't want to be that person. Somehow there'd been a mistake. I kept feeling that. The door would open, Jack and my mother would be there, and I'd tell that officer to go fuck himself and then I'd go home. That's what a part of me felt. But the other part of me, the part that saw the room with my eyes, that heard the whir of the cameras, that part told me there were feelings I had to push away, that from now on I had to kill what I feel. It was a part I'd felt all my life.

iii > > >

The next day they changed my room. We went down to the equipment room before breakfast, they had me dress in a blue uniform made of cloth, and then we walked up a set of back stairs to the third floor. This new room was a real cell. Bars were across the front, and the other three walls were made of concrete. It wasn't all that small either. It was bigger than all the cells I'd seen in the movies. It had a sink, a toilet, and a little bed. It even had a window. High above, up near the ceiling was a tiny window. If I stood on the bed I could see out. I don't think they ever figured they'd have someone so tall. There were no bars on it either. I forget the name, but the pane was made of that hard plastic stuff. The plastic was kind of hazy, but through it I could see lots of blue sky, the snow on some roofs, bare trees, and a kind of outdoor court down below. At one end of the court was a basketball hoop. I saw that right away. It had one of those chain metal nets around the rim.

No one else was up here with me. There was a whole row of cells up here like mine, but all of them were empty. In the early mornings, through my window, I saw men in the courtyard down below. Sometimes in the visiting room when I went, the men were there too, dressed in blue like I was, but always they'd be hustled out before I went in. I asked Jack why, and he said it was for my own protection. He said that Brewster was a relatively small town. But I didn't mind being alone, I didn't. I liked my cell a lot better than the white room they had me in at first, with no windows. There was a camera up here as well, but it was out in the hall above the bars. If I got on my bed I was out of sight. So it was a lot better. It was up here too that I realized I was in jail, or at least as much as I could. But my mind wouldn't let it sink in. I mean only a few days after I got up here, I started to dream about basketball every night. And I don't mean just dream either, but I was out on the court playing it, feeling it, hearing the people in the bleachers go wild. I tried to stop myself. I didn't want to give it up, but in a way it hurt too much. When my eyes opened, when I woke up, everything just stopped. The concrete returned, and the sink, and then that little square of light up on the wall across from my window. It was then I knew I was in jail, not by what I saw I mean, by the way I woke up, but by my battle inside to stop my mind. And Amanda. No shit. At the beginning, when I was finally left alone, I beat off about every five minutes thinking of Amanda. I couldn't stop it. All during the night I beat off. I would've given anything to touch her skin again, to put my lips on her lips, on her nipples, to even smell her breath. And trying to stop all that, that's when a big part of me realized I was in a jail.

During the day though, I didn't have much time to think. Me and Jack and Danny, we were usually pretty busy. And the trial was set to begin early, only three months away. I was surprised, I remember O.J. had something like a year and a half to wait before his. So when Jack and Danny found out the date, they turned up the pressure a couple of notches.

Since the state had no law against it, Jack tried to get the judge to allow TV in the courtroom. He said it could only work to our advantage. The more coverage we got, and the more people saw me for who I was, the more questions they would ask themselves.

That kind of thing, he said, always found a way of filtering into a jury, even a sequestered jury. But this judge was tough, Jack said, very traditional and inflexible. He only gave us a 40/60 chance of getting coverage. So when Judge McLaughlin decided he would allow a limited-angle coverage in the courtroom, of his bench, of the witness stand, and of the defense and prosecution tables, Jack came back in the office and just screamed his lungs out. He said the coverage would be immense, that CNN, Court TV, the American Justice Channel, they were all signing on and working themselves into a frenzy already. He called it a national media phenomenon. Then him and Danny talked about going out to buy me some clothes, about dressing me right. Some days I'd wear a sharp-looking navy blue blazer, they said, depending on what was on the docket. Other days, they'd want to dress me in what they called the Ivy League look: a tweed jacket with a V-neck sweater and tie, probably in rust tones, because they were completely passive and went good with my natural coloring.

Those first two weeks I saw a couple more psychiatrists. Jack and Danny flew them in from New York City and California. One guy was Chinese and spoke English with a strong accent, but they said he was an expert though. Jack wanted to see if we could use them to testify on our behalf. I met with them every day, for long periods of time. They always tried to hide what they were talking about, but it was pretty obvious. They asked me if my biological father had ever touched me, if Sidney'd ever touched me, if my mother had ever touched me, or kissed me on the lips, or slept with me in the same bed. I could've I suppose, some of it was kind of sick, but I didn't get upset. I knew they were just doing their job, trying to find something to help our case.

But Jack and Danny dug away at me pretty good too. They asked me if I'd ever been a member of a satanic cult. If I'd ever been even remotely associated with any kind of cult, that could help us greatly. Anything I'd experienced that could prove outside control, they said, juries nowadays usually ate that stuff right up. They jumped at the chance to deflect the blame from society. I had to say no. Then, another time, they asked me if someone had been sleeping with my girlfriend. That was an excellent one, they said. If they could somehow bring adolescent love and passion into the equation, juries were always sympathetic. I had to say no to that one too. After a while, they got very frustrated. They said they were trying to help me, but I was giving them nothing. They needed that one little personal hook to grab on to, to tip the scales. I didn't want to, I don't tell anyone, but I told them I had A.D.D. They both looked at me then, real serious at first, and then they burst right out laughing, hard, bent right over there in the office. When they could talk again, they just said they hardly thought a jury would consider that attenuating.

One day, after breakfast but a lot later than usual, my officer came to get me. He brought me down to the office. On the way, at a place where magazines usually are, I saw a newspaper on the table. It was one of those you buy at a supermarket check-out. It caught my eye right off because I was on the front page. But I'd seen me on *Newsweek* and on other newspapers, so it wasn't my picture that made me look. My face was real mean on this one, snarling. Somehow, they'd got hold of the photo from the local newspaper, the one where I'm dunking the ball, and they'd cut everything out except for the face. Then they'd added this body building body to it, strapped an ammo belt across the chest, and there I was standing with this real mean snarl, toting an m-16. Above my face, in big letters, were the words, "ALL-AMERICAN BOY MASSACRES ENTIRE HIGH SCHOOL!" I stopped and stared. It wasn't me. I was in jail, I knew that. I was going to be on trial, I knew that too. A big part of me knew why, I think. But the person in that picture wasn't me.

When I walked into the office that morning, one of the psychiatrists was there. Me, Jack and Danny, we'd never been in the
same room with a psychiatrist before. I'd always been alone with
them. Jack looked a bit surprised when he saw me.

"Philip," he said, "I didn't expect you until a little later."

I could see he was uneasy, didn't really want me there just then.
I told him I could leave and come back.

"No, that's all right," he said. "It's probably a good thing
you're here. We'll discuss this openly. If I ever have you take the
stand, this is something you need to be aware of." He looked back
down at Dr. Thao, the Chinese psychiatrist. "As you were beginning to say, Dr. Thao, the tendencies were schizoid . . ."

"Are you sure?" Dr. Thao said, looking up at me.

"Sure," Jack said.

"Schizoid narcissistic," Dr. Thao said. "The boy has definite
and strong schizoid narcissistic tendencies."

"Meaning?"

"Meaning that he tends to center his existence within himself,
to be preoccupied with himself, and to pay little attention to the
rest of the world other than for his own benefit."

"Well is it strong enough, detrimental enough for what we
need? Could we get some good mileage out of it?"

"Doubtful," Dr. Thao said.

"Why?"

"Because, I'm afraid, that also more or less defines the whole
country for the last few decades or so. A jury would have a difficult time appreciating the aberrant aspects of something so close
to their own experience."

"Maybe," Jack said, "but it's just what we need. I mean it
sounds great. Especially the schizoid. But if we ever decided to
use it, is there any way we can get rid of the narcissistic? People
hear narcissistic and they think selfish. Automatic. And selfish is

definitely not an idea we want to get across in this case. I don't know, is there any way we can drop the narcissistic and add a maniacal to it, or a delusional, something like that. Is that possible?"

Dr. Thao just shrugged his shoulders.

"It is what it is," he said.

"Well, thanks a lot for coming all this way, Doctor," Jack said, holding out his hand as Dr. Thao stood. "We appreciate it. Consider the check already in the mail."

"Oh, by the way," Dr. Thao said, looking up as he was closing his briefcase, "do you mind paying me with a bank money order?"

Jack smiled, glancing over to Danny.

"No, of course not," he said. "A money order it is."

Dr. Thao kind of bowed, said thank you, and left.

"Well, have a seat, Philip," Jack then said, pointing at the table, "we've got a lot to discuss this morning."

He pulled up a chair. As always, Danny stood behind him.

"So, first of all," he said, "we may as well discuss the reports we have from the two psychiatrists." He opened a folder and spread a bunch of printouts on the table. "And I'm not going to lie to you Philip, but both psychiatrists said remarkably similar things. We've got some work to do if we ever want you to take the stand. These are tendencies that Danny and I have observed in you as well, but it seems they become even more pronounced when you're questioned directly about what happened. For example, they both say that you're incredibly detached, lucid, and willing to talk. One of them states, and I quote, 'At times he talks as if it were another who committed the act.'" Jack looked up from the table. "So, do you have anything to say about that comment, Philip? Can you enlighten us on any of this?"

I just shrugged my shoulders. I could feel Jack frustrated. Danny stepped forward.

"Look, Philip," he said — his voice was almost angry —"there are certain things in your behavior we're going to have to try to explain to a jury, and you have to help us. I mean this is an incredibly violent and bloody act we're talking about. Being clear and lucid, and at the same time being the one who pulled the trigger, this is not going to help our case. It will play right into the Prosecution's hands. The one fact they're going to pound into that jury, over and over, is that after the first burst of anger or delusion or whatever it was, and three people already lay there dead, then you began what the police describe as 'target shooting.' You stood there in that hallway, and aimed and fired until your clip was empty, coldly picking people off all the way down." Danny's voice rose even more, angry. His face flushed red, bright red. "Now for fucksakes, Philip, help us out here! They're going to jump right on this fucking lucidity shit and kill us with it! Can't you see that?! This will be their proof that you did this coldly, clearly, with premeditation! So show some emotion for fucksakes! Show some remorse! Make it fucking up if you have to! We don't care! I mean they're gonna plaster that fucking courtroom with the most gory, the most violent pictures you've ever seen, and you can't be sitting there like some fucking sphinx! Because if you do, that'll be it! No shit! Game over!"

Danny just dropped his hands and stood there in the middle of the floor. Jack had a hand over his face.

"Look," I said, "it's only so violent because I did it."

"Excuse me?" Jack said, looking out between his fingers.

"I mean think about it," I said. "It's only so violent because you know me, and I'm the one who did it. I mean if you'd like seen it on TV or in a movie, it wouldn't seem all that violent to you. Or at least it would for a while, but it wouldn't last I mean. Because . . ."

"Philip," Jack said, real stern, "you better stop yourself right there."

"No listen," I said, "let me explain. I know it was violent, and it was wrong to do. I hate seeing those people dead, I do, but it wasn't all that violent. What about those kids in Kentucky, for example? I mean they ambushed a whole school and did it on purpose. They killed and wounded a lot more than I did. And they did it on purpose too. And then that kid in that Christian school, you remember? He walked down the hall when everyone was praying and shot them all in the head. I didn't do that. So do you see what I mean? It's only so violent because you know me, because you're here. If you were some place else reading about it you might feel upset for a few minutes, but it wouldn't really bother your day. You'd still go to work, you'd still have a home and a wife and kids and stuff, because it's not close to you, it ain't you, and you see lots more violent stuff than that all the time."

Jack just stared at me. Danny too. For a long time they just stared.

"Holy shit," Danny then said, real quiet. He turned his eyes away. "Wrong plea."

"No," Jack said, looking down at the table. "No. But at least he's answered the question on whether we'll have him take the stand or not."

"No shit."

"And we didn't hear any of that, did we?"

"No, we didn't."

I left only a few minutes after. And ever since that day there was a change between us. I don't know what happened, but me and Danny and Jack, we never laughed and joked again like we did before that day. And we used to laugh and joke a lot. They're really funny guys. But something happened. They were always real serious then, even when the same things came up that made us laugh before. I knew why deep down though, I'm not stupid. So after that day I just decided to keep everything I think to myself.

My mother came in to see me every day. Just after lunch, my officer led me into the visitor's room, and Mom would already be in there, at the same table. After she got to the point where she didn't have to cry anymore, we gradually talked about just plain normal things. We even talked about the future. She said that every year she'd buy me this certain kind of IRA, and that way I would have a nice little nest egg when I got out. We only had a half hour too, but we talked about a lot of things, things we never talked about before. And my mother can be pretty. I'd never noticed that. Some days she was in there waiting with like these silk scarves on, these dresses, and she looked really pretty.

Then one day, in the middle of the afternoon, I was led down to the visiting room. Through the glass I saw Coach inside. I don't know why, but I didn't want him there at all. I felt almost mad. It was strange. He stood when I walked in the door and shook my hand. He was real nervous. He asked me how I was doing. Then he didn't say anything. He looked around. He rubbed his thighs. He was real nervous. Then he said how the much the team missed me, how they'd only won three games since I'd left, how they might not even make the tournament now, when before they'd been picked to be number one. At the end he made this real high nervous laugh. I didn't want him to be there. Then he leaned a little more towards the glass, even more nervous. He said that if there was ever anything he could do for me to just ask, that he would do anything for me, that I was a great kid, that he loved me like his own son. I was surprised when he said that. I didn't like it. I didn't want to hear it. I didn't say anything. I just wanted him to leave. And after a few more words then, he did.

Most of the time, when I wasn't with Danny and Jack, I was alone in my cell. For the first week I remember I hated to go back up there alone, with nothing to do. Then I started to look forward to it. There was no one reason why, but I just got less and less bored. I'd always liked things intense, coming in fast, a lot at a time. That's just the way it was out there. But after being with Jack and Danny, I couldn't wait to come back up here, to sit on my bed, and to watch the light kind of move its way across the far wall. I know it sounds stupid, it must, but it calmed everything down inside of me. It opened something, and I just felt closer. To what, I don't know. And I didn't beat off as much either. I still did a lot, but I didn't have to do it, if you know what I mean.

Every afternoon too I'd hear the men down in the courtyard. I'd stand up on my bed and watch them down there, just walking around or playing basketball. I would've given anything to go down there and shoot around for a few minutes. I'd been there over two weeks and I hadn't gotten to go outside even once yet. So one day I mentioned it to Jack. He seemed pretty pissed off about it. And he must've said something, because the next day, at three-thirty, my officer came up with this real growl on his face and asked me who I got down on my knees and blew this time. He said I was to have a half hour of free time outside every afternoon. Then, when we got downstairs, a basketball was sitting in the doorway.

It just about killed the son of a bitch to hand the ball over to me. Then, I can't begin to explain what I felt when I took the ball outside and started to dribble, started to drive towards that basket. I didn't care if it was twenty below out. I didn't care if there was snow piled all over the place. I didn't even care if the stupid net was made of metal. I was like flying. And I shot and drove, and drove and dunked, and jump-shot and drove. Michael Jordan, Karl Malone, Shaquille O'Neal, they were all stunned by my overwhelming superiority. It was just so cool. And I was gonna be out there every afternoon from now on too, that's what I couldn't believe. I was gonna be out there every afternoon for a whole half hour.

iv > > >

I don't know when I started to remember. I was up there in my cell alone so much, I guess there was just no way to avoid it. I remembered stuff I did when I was a little kid. I remembered teachers I hadn't thought about ever. I remembered my room. When I sat on my bed, after lights out, I would walk my eyes real slow all around my room at home. I'd try to pick out every single detail. And each time when I thought that was it, that I'd remembered everything, something I'd missed would pop into my mind a few minutes later, or in the middle of talking to Jack, or especially during my sleep.

And the idea of time. Something happened. I can't exactly say what. But nothing went forward. There were things I did, spaces I filled, like lunch, basketball, seeing Jack and Danny, but time only existed because of the things I did. It was like one of those ideas that come into your head sometimes when you're stoned, but I wasn't stoned. Time didn't exist, and never could, never did, not without things to build it.

Then one day I heard two sets of footsteps come up the back stairs. Except for my officer, no one ever came up to my cell. And when the hall door opened, I saw him walk in with Reverend Mitchell. Reverend Mitchell is the minister from the Brewster Congregational Church. He used to be my Boy Scout troop leader

too. We used to have the meetings right down in the church basement. And I was always a bit nervous with him as my troop leader.
I always thought he wanted to talk about God. I mean that's why
people become ministers in the first place, they want to talk about
God. And so when he took us on camping trips, or taught us how
to tie knots, I always felt in a way that he was just biding his time,
that what he really wanted to do was talk about God.

"You have a visitor," my officer said.

He slid open the bars. Reverend Mitchell held out a hand. His
smile was too big, too much. I felt uneasy. But I realized how hard
it was.

"Philip," he said, "how are you doing?"

It was in the afternoon, almost time for basketball. I didn't
want to say too much. My officer stayed out in the hall, the bars
open. Reverend Mitchell sat beside me on the bed. He was nervous. Everyone who came to see me was nervous. He said he was
on his way to the hospital and decided to drop in. He said my
mother seemed to be doing better, that she certainly looked forward to her daily visits with me. He smiled, and said I'd never
believe the amount of cakes and cookies that the women from
church had offered either, but that he'd had to turn down because
of the policy here. He said too there were a lot of people praying
for me. Then his face got real serious. He asked me if I would pray
with him. He reached out and took my hand. I'd never held a
man's hand before, not since I was little. I didn't like it. Then
he started to cry, not out loud, but in his voice. It broke. I didn't
expect it. He said he couldn't imagine what a young man of my
caliber must be feeling, the pain, the torture I must be putting
myself through. It was nearly time for basketball. I could see that
because of the square of light up on the wall, across from the window. Then he said God would see me through this. God would
give me the answers I must be so desperately seeking. Then he

prayed. He squeezed my hand. I watched the square on the wall get dimmer. When he was done, he squeezed my hand again. "There," he said, "now I'm sure you'll feel so much better."

I got two letters from Amanda. In the first one she said she loved me, wanted to have my children now more than ever, and would wait for me her entire life if she had to. In the second one she said she still loved me, and would love me until the day she died, but couldn't write anymore because her parents wouldn't let her.

But her smell was on the letters. I don't know what happened. I couldn't beat off enough. I'd wait till the smell was fresh again. Maybe ten minutes, maybe fifteen minutes, until I could smell again. I just couldn't beat off enough. All over the letters. It was crazy. I don't know what happened.

One day, after lunch, I was in the visitor's room waiting for my mother when my mother didn't come in. Instead, my biological father did. I was surprised. I'd imagined it before, him walking in through the door, but I hadn't seen myself so glad, I don't think. I didn't know I still could be. He stood and hugged me for a long time. My officer let him. Then we sat at the table, and he told me he would be with me every day until the trial was over, that he'd taken a place in town and would stay here for as long as he had to. He said I looked good, pale but good. Then he told me about his place back in Minnesota, and it was like he was making it up. I wanted him to stop his lying. Then, towards the end, he broke down too. I knew he would. He blamed himself, his lack of this, his lack of that, his pent-up rage, his cowardice, the goddamn war. But I knew he would. It's always there. He has to blame something. When I was ten he screamed in that kitchen. He walked back and forth day and night and he screamed. He hated, he just hated. I couldn't know why then. I was only ten.

During the third week, jury selection began. When it did, me and Jack and Danny, we all sat in the courtroom with the Prosecution and we interviewed people. It was strange. The people didn't have names, only numbers. Twelve regular jurors and six alternates had to be chosen. The Prosecution asked complicated questions. Jack asked just very simple questions. Real simple. What they thought of the weather we were having. If they had children. If they preferred meat or fish, that was one he asked. The Prosecution was really thrown by that one too. I never could figure it out either.

A lot of the people knew who I was because of basketball. They'd seen me on TV or in the newspaper. Most of them were dismissed right off by the Prosecution. For a long time, like for three entire weeks, us and the Prosecution could agree only on two or three people. But Jack said not to worry, that it was in the Prosecution's interest to get the trial under way as soon as possible, and to reach that end they would compromise rather quickly. He was right. He never came right out and said it, not outside of our meetings, but Jack wanted at least seven women on the jury, with at least three of them over the age of forty-five, and he got them. Until that point though, everyone fought all the time and acted pissed off, but in the end he got exactly what he wanted. And I guess, at least according to Jack, the Prosecution did too.

Jason wrote me. It was a strange letter. He talked about waiting in the car, about hearing the shots, about driving around all night as fast as he could and wanting to disappear, and then just driving off over a bank and into the lake, hoping he would drown. But the goddamn lake was frozen. I only read it once.

Then one morning, when I was with Jack and Danny, a different officer came in and told me someone was waiting in the visitor's room. It was ten-thirty in the morning and real cold outside, real windy. Upstairs, I'd heard the wind howl all night long. I thought it was my biological father, he didn't have a special time to come yet. From the corridor outside the visitor's room though,

I saw her blond hair through the glass. She had a light blue sweater on. I don't know what I felt. Or I know but I can't explain it. When the officer opened the door, she looked up from the table. She seemed surprised. She just looked at me. Her face tried to smile, but real timid.

"Hi, Philip," she said.

I didn't know what to do. I was dressed in my old blue uniform. She was so pretty. Her sweater was this light blue and fluffy stuff, real soft. I just stood there. She sat on her side of the glass. She told me my mother called and asked her to come. She said she'd wanted to come anyway, but didn't know if they'd let her.

"Your mother had to say I was still your girlfriend."

I still don't think I talked. I'd forgotten what I feel like when I see her. It just runs through me, around me. She was so pretty. And I call it pretty because that's the only word I have, but it's so much more than that. It's like if I tried to touch her she would just disappear. She said some things about the high school, about Amanda. Then she went quiet, and I could see she was going to cry too. For some reason, everyone cries. She fought it real hard. Then something in her broke and she looked up at me, right straight at me. Her words came from some place so deep, so sincere, it was like she thought them to me, like no sound ever came from her lips but I felt them. They were my own. She said she missed me so much. She said that since we'd broken up it was like she was wandering inside, lost, that no matter how hard she tried or who she went out with it was always there, this emptiness. They were exactly my own.

"God, I love you," she then said. "I can't help it. I just love you."

Then she said this was all her fault. If she'd had the courage to fight for our love, to resist her parents, to convince them how much she loved me, none of this would've happened. Deep down she was sure of this. I wanted to say no, but I didn't want the sound of my voice to spoil the sound of hers. I don't think I talked at all. I couldn't, didn't have to. When she left, I had like this beam of light in me. That sounds stupid, I know, but it came from deep inside somewhere and went all the way through me, solid, warm. And after that morning I didn't feel the same. I can't explain it either, but after that morning I didn't feel alone.

The closer the trial came, the more everyone around me got nervous. The officers, Jack and Danny, the guys who brought in my food, everyone. It showed up in the way they moved, the way they talked. Their eyes never looked at mine any more, or if they did, it was real quick and then away. I wished they wouldn't do that. It wasn't necessary. I didn't know why they couldn't look at me like before. I mentioned it to Jack. He said it was because most everyone around here had come to really like me, that it was only normal, just human nature, that they should begin to get nervous. I don't know if I believed him.

A week before the trial there was some last-minute wrangling. Jack explained it to me. The Prosecution tried to limit the jury to choosing between five to ten years for some kind of manslaughter, or the death penalty, just those two choices. When they did that, Jack just laughed right out loud in the courtroom. Luckily, I guess, at least according to Jack, Judge McLaughlin did too. He was real pissed off, and instead, he opened up every possible option to the jury, seven in all, including the fifteen- to twenty-year one Jack had told me about when he first got here. Jack and Danny were real happy about that decision, real excited. The day before the trial, they brought in like this huge Chinese dinner and we all sat around and stuffed ourselves. It was a great meal, and Jack and Danny tried to laugh and crack jokes all the way through, but anyone could tell they were nervous.

V > > >

The trial began in mid-April. Through my cell window, the trees had just come out with little buds. The sky had changed too, and the clouds. The sky was a lighter, more faded blue, and the clouds looked more like the clouds of summer. The trial began on a Tuesday, at nine o'clock. When me and Jack and Danny walked up the ramp towards the courthouse, I saw the crowd down below through the glass. It filled the street. TV vans were parked all over the place down there. Lots of people looked up, pointed, and then ran towards the courthouse. Cameras were everywhere on shoulders.

The courthouse lobby was noisy, jammed with people who shouted questions. I didn't look up. Cameras flashed all around me. I was dressed in a navy blue blazer, a blue shirt and grey slacks, and a grey silk tie. Jack and Danny had told Mom what to buy for clothes, and they were very expensive I think. An hour before, Jack had tied the knot for my tie, and it was real thin, with this little dimple like just below it. It was definitely the sharpest looking knot I've ever seen. Mom came over to the station, and she couldn't get over how handsome I was. She was real nervous though. Everybody was nervous. Danny didn't want to even talk. It reminded me of the lockerroom last year, before our championship game. No one could speak. Everyone's face was pale. The only difference was that some of the guys threw up.

The courtroom was full of people. I'd never been in there with the pews all filled. It changed the whole room. It was just like you see it on TV, only a lot brighter. When the officer opened the door, everyone was quiet at first, but then they all turned and whispered. They watched us as we walked down the aisle towards our table. Jack was dressed real sharp. He obviously knew what to wear. He'd looked like some kind of a clown over there at the police station, out of place, but here in the browns and the bright lights of the courtroom he looked real sharp. Danny was dressed in green, but Danny always dressed in green. On the right, the Prosecution was already seated at their table. Their laptop computers were open, and stacks of documents were piled in front of them. They didn't look when we walked in. Above them, over there on the wall above where the jurors would sit, was the only TV camera allowed in the courtroom. It had a metal bar across one side, to limit where it could turn.

We sat down, and a few minutes later the jurors came in through a side door. Seven women and five men. I'd seen them so much during selection, that I knew them all by heart. They were all nervous too. When Judge McLaughlin came in we all stood, and then things got underway.

To give their opening statement, the Prosecution chose one of the two women on their team, Rachel King. Jack had told me they'd use her as the front person. For what they wanted to achieve, he said, having a woman up there was in general much more effective. She was small, had short dark hair, and always dressed in dark blues and whites. She was really built too. I wasn't supposed to notice that I know, but she was. I thought of her up there in my cell sometimes.

Jack had told me to get myself ready, to take what the Prosecution would say with a grain of salt, and to not even listen if I could stop myself. I tried for a minute or two, to stop myself,

but I couldn't. I don't think it's all that natural, not when someone talks about you. Rachel King said that the case was black and
white. It would be crystal clear when all the evidence was in,
when all the witnesses had had their say, that the Defendant had
acted in a deliberate and premeditated fashion, in fact, in the
most wanton, cold-blooded fashion that a human being can act.
They, the jurors, would see the physical and emotional devasta-
tion this act had caused. They would see the maliciousness, the
deliberate and scheming maliciousness concealed beneath this
young man's rather pleasant exterior (she was pointing at me).
And when they did, they would have no trouble whatsoever in
agreeing on the one, the one and only just sentence, that fit the
atrocity of this crime.

I'd expected a lot more. I knew it was only an opening statement, but at O.J.'s trial they'd talked for half the day. Then Jack
got up and spoke. He went over to the jury, rested his hand
on the rail, and talked like they were just all sitting in his kitchen.
But his was short too. He said the boy had openly pleaded guilty
(he called me a boy), and it was on their shoulders now to render
a just sentence. He said he realized the horrendous nature of
the crime, but then he looked at each one and asked if they really
knew the true nature of this boy? He threw his arms wide and said
dozens of people had volunteered, had actually called him and
volunteered, wanting to go up there on that stand (he pointed
to the witness stand) and testify to the sterling character of this
young man (he called me a young man). And this, might he add,
in the very same town where such a crime had been committed.
He looked at each one of them then, slowly nodding his head,
and said, "That is unheard of. I mean such a gesture is unheard of.
Now, you tell me if something isn't way out of synch here." He
turned halfway around, took a step away, and then turned back.
He set one hand back on the rail. "No, we're not trying to conceal

anything in this matter, and certainly not the ugliness of this act. But that boy sitting over there (he pointed at me again), in no way would it serve any notion of justice should your decision be to deliver him up for execution by the state. For let us not mince our words, this is why we're here, this is what it all comes down to, and we know it. There would be no trial at all if the Prosecution didn't want this boy put to death."

Rachel King shot up then, exploded, shouting something about inflammatory. Judge McLaughlin grabbed his gavel. Jack turned and bowed, politely, as if to say he was sorry. Then he turned back to the jurors.

"But you will see that bad decisions were made, bad influences were absorbed, and circumstances then came together at a point where, for some indecipherable reason, a basically very good boy committed a terrible crime."

There was no afternoon session that first day. The Prosecution asked for a recess to ready the courtroom. And when we all walked back into the courtroom the next day, it was like Danny had said. Down front on big stands, flashed overhead on a big screen, were huge photos of the crime scene. They were in color. People were up there lying on a floor, covered in blood. One, a police officer, still had his eyes open. When we walked in, people cried in the courtroom. The photos looked like the picture of an airport I saw in a magazine once. A terrorist had blown up an airport, in Israel or France or someplace, and bodies and blood were everywhere. Or like in this Arnold Schwarzennager movie, I forget which one, but in this big scene at the end with everyone massacred at his feet. When the jurors came in, two of the women, number 5 and number 11, put their hands to their mouths and had to leave. They came back in later, but all pale and shaking.

The Prosecution called their first witness. It was Detective Kimball, the short detective with slick-backed hair who looked like

an Italian. Rachel King asked him to describe the crime scene, exactly what we were seeing in the photos. She gave him a pointer,
and he left the stand and walked to each picture, describing and
pointing. He used all their names. He said how they were killed.
A bullet exploding in the officer's thigh, and severing the artery;
another entering the girl's abdomen, as yet another pierced her
lungs; another exploding round fired directly into the second
officer's chest, causing the massive damage we saw there on the
screen; another entering the boy's sides at the ribs, piercing the
lungs, and exiting a shoulder. The courtroom was dead silent.
Jack and Danny didn't move. Then the detective went through
all the pictures of those who were wounded. Two more jurors
had to leave, a man and a woman, number 3 and number 7. When
the detective was finished, the screen overhead was turned off,
but all the other photos stayed where they were. Jack didn't have
any questions.

The Prosecution called another witness. It was my principal,
Mr. Babcock. He had on a sportcoat, but over where his hand
should be there was a black glove. Rachel King first asked him
about his injury. He said a bullet hit him in the arm, a special kind
of sonic bullet the doctors had said, and it had completely shattered his bone from the shoulder to the wrist. Rachel King made
him stop, made him repeat the kind of bullet it was. She nodded
and said, "I see." Then she told him to continue. Mr. Babcock said
that from the elbow down they had had to amputate. They were
waiting for the swelling to go down so they could fit him with
a permanent prophylactic device. He said it all with no emotion
too, just the way he always talked at school. Then she asked him
about the day itself. He said he'd heard there was a gun in a locker.
He also said he'd heard it was in mine and couldn't believe it,
but Ms. King reminded him to just recount the facts as they
happened, please, not his beliefs. He called the police, they came,

and they went down to investigate. "And when we were halfway down," he said, "Philip just turned on us and started shooting."

"With no provocation?"

"Objection," Jack said, standing; "leading the witness."

"Sustained," Judge McLaughlin said. "Rephrase the question, please."

Rachel King took a deep breath.

"Mr. Babcock, when you were approaching the defendant, in your best recollection, what was your posture?"

"We were just walking normally," Mr. Babcock said.

"Was this your first time walking down the high school corridor with police officers?"

"Unfortunately not. I'm afraid it happens all too often nowadays, for whatever reason."

"And would you say you were walking in the same manner as you always walk, I mean when accompanied by police officers."

"Yes."

"Thank you. No further questions, Your Honor."

Jack stood up. He asked Mr. Babcock if he or the police had made any menacing gestures. Had they shouted, had the police been reaching for their weapons, anything like that? Mr. Babcock said no, and Jack said thank you as well.

At lunch break, despite all the photos that he said were very effectively presented, Jack felt good. He said my principal had a definitely biased interpretation of the events leading up to the act, and Jack thought he could easily score some quick points because of that.

After lunch, the Prosecution called one of the janitors from the school. Rachel King asked him about his duties at school, and then asked him what he was doing on the day of the shooting. He said he was working out in the hall, trying to open a locker that was jammed. She told him to recount what he saw that day. He said he saw Mr. Babcock and the police turn the corner and start walking up the corridor. He could see they were looking farther up, so he turned and looked up that way himself. He said he saw the boy pull a gun from his locker, and just start shooting. He ducked into a room, but watched through a side window. He said that after the boy had shot the two policemen and Mr. Babcock, he just kept on firing. He just stood there, and real calm, he picked everyone off up and down the corridor.

When Rachel King sat, Jack stood. He told the janitor that he would like to take him back through the events of that morning again, but slowly this time, "and please try to recollect as best you can."

Rachel King stood. She objected. This was not a witness for the Defense, she said, and Counselor Shapiro was certainly not limiting himself to a cross-examination. The Judge overruled. He said this was not a trial to prove guilt or innocence, that had already been decided, and in the name of expediency he would give both sides a great deal of leeway in their questioning. She was pissed. She requested a side-bar. The judge denied her, saying there was no reason for it, and to move things along. She was really pissed. She just stood there. The judge told her that if she stood there any longer, then she better grab her checkbook and start writing out a five-hundred-dollar check, because that was what she'd be paying for her contempt. She sat down. Jack continued. He asked the janitor about when he first saw Mr. Babcock and the police. What were their facial expressions, what was their posture. "Were they at all menacing in any way?"

"Objection, Your Honor," Rachel King said, standing; "leading the witness."

"Sustained. Rephrase the question, Mr. Shapiro."

Jack thought for a moment.

"The police officers, for example," he then said. "Let's take their hands first of all, where were their hands when you saw them?"

"Their hands?" the janitor said. He shrugged his shoulders.

"Yes. Were they in the air, down by their sides? To your best recollection, where were they?"

The janitor thought. Then he put a right hand on his hip.

"Both of the cops, the police officers, had their hands on their hips, like this."

"Would you stand and turn towards the jury, please, and show them what you mean."

The janitor stood with his right hand on his hip.

"Like this," he said.

"Now," Jack said, "to your best recollection, what was on the right hip?"

The janitor shrugged.

"A gun I guess."

Rachel King shot up again.

"Objection, Your Honor. The witness is not qualified to answer."

The judge just kind of glanced her way. He rolled his eyes.

"Ms. King," he said, "I think the man perhaps knows what a gun looks like, don't you? Overruled."

"So," Jack said, "according to your best recollection, they had their right hands in contact with their guns, on their hips, but in contact with their guns."

"Objection," Rachel King said again, "misstating the witness."

The judge turned towards the witness.

"Is that what you mean, sir," he said, "that their right hands were on their hips, touching the guns?"

"Yes," the janitor said. "You know, with the palm like kind of down over it."

"Continue, Mr. Shapiro," the judge said.

"And did you hear anything as they walked down the corridor. Anything at all? Did either the principal or the police officers speak?"

The janitor was thinking.

"Now that you mention it," he said, "someone said something, I think."

"What did they say?"

"I can't remember."

"Well, was it in a normal tone of voice, a shouted tone of voice? Can you remember how it was said?"

"Yes," the janitor said. "It was definitely shouted. I don't know what was said, and I don't know who said it either, but it was definitely shouted."

"Now, to your best recollection, where did it come from?"

"From them," he said.

"Who are you calling 'them'?" Jack said.

"Those three guys," the janitor said.

"The two police officers and Mr. Babcock, the principal?"

"Yes."

Jack hesitated. He thought and slightly nodded his head. He tapped just the tips of his fingers together real slow.

"Now," he then said, "let me see if I have your testimony right. You saw the principal, Mr. Babcock, and the two police officers walking down the corridor; the two police officers had their hands on their hips, in contact with their weapons; and someone, you can't say who, but one of those three, shouted. Is that right?"

The janitor nodded. Danny reached over and patted me on the arm.

"No further questions, Your Honor," Jack said.

The trial moved along real fast, a lot faster than I expected. O.J.'s trial had lasted a year and a half. I mentioned that to Jack.

He just said it was obvious they didn't have Judge McLaughlin. And I don't think Judge McLaughlin allowed even one side-bar the whole time. In O.J.'s trial, that Japanese judge, I forget his name, he held a side-bar every time you turned around.

By the third day, Jack said the Prosecution was over halfway through their presentation already. I was never allowed to know any of the witnesses that would be called, either for the Prosecution or for the Defense. Jack knew, he had a list, but he said it would be better for me and for the team if I didn't know in advance.

On the afternoon of the third day, the Prosecution called Jason to the stand. He was real nervous. He didn't want to do it. He felt rotten, I could tell. But I didn't care, I knew he had to. He told them about me bringing him over to my uncle's to see the gun, about me bringing the gun to school, and then about calling me at home so I'd go to the high school and take it out. Rachel King made him repeat that three or four times, about how he called me over and over to take the gun out.

When she was finished, Jack stood. He asked Jason whose idea it was in the first place to go over and see the gun. Jason said it was his, that I'd told him about my uncle's guns a lot of times, and that he'd always wanted to go over and have a look. And whose idea was it to bring this specific gun to the high school? Jason didn't know. He just said it was both of our idea. Had we thought about the consequences with the administration, especially with all the commotion about guns in school nowadays? Jason said he didn't at the time, but that night he got to thinking about it, how dangerous it could be, and he called me up. And what did I say? I said that I'd take it out. Then Jack asked Jason how long he'd known me. Jason said all his life. He asked Jason if he could tell when I was not being myself, when I was lying, for example. And here, Rachel King shot up again and objected, saying the witness was not clairvoyant, after all. The judge thought a minute, then overruled, but warned Jack to end that line of questioning right there, to restrict himself to this one question. Jack asked Jason again if he thought he could tell when I was not being myself, when I was lying. Jason said he guessed so, and Jack asked him if he felt I was being sincere, did he feel I was telling the truth when I told him I was going to take the gun out of my locker? Jason said yes, but he kept on calling me and said he knew he'd have to keep on calling me anyway, because that's the way I was, I was always thinking about basketball. Either that or schoolwork. So having to call me wasn't nothing new. During basketball season especially, he said, he was used to saying the same thing over and over to me about a hundred times before it sunk in. Some people in the courtroom laughed at that. Jack laughed too. It was the only time anyone laughed.

The next question Jack asked Jason was what he was doing when the shooting took place. Jason said he was waiting for me out in the school parking lot, that I was supposed to take the gun out of the locker and bring it right out to the car. Jack acted like this was a real revelation, that me and Jason were planning at that very minute to take the gun back home in the car. And he left it right there like that, hanging. That was the last question he asked.

On the fourth day the Prosecution brought up the two wives of the police officers. They cried, could hardly speak. They talked about their husbands, what they'd been like, about the children they'd left behind. Rachel King would pour them water, pass them tissues. Jack said it was all very well done, all very well choreographed. But they were upset too though, really upset. And all around them, those photos were still there in the court-room. I don't know how they could've done it, those wives I mean. It must have been hard. Jack asked them no questions.

Then a woman came in who was the mother of one of the kids

that died, a freshman, Billy Jenkins. He was one of those dark spots a ways down the corridor, Rachel King said, pointing to the largest photo, down there slumped against a locker, a bullet through his lungs, "that's Billy Jenkins." I never knew him. I didn't even remember ever seeing him before. His mother cried too. She said she was divorced, that Billy was her only child. Then she just talked about him, what he liked in life, what he planned to do, stuff like that. The courtroom was real quiet. Over in the jury box the men just stared. A lot of the women just looked down. Jack asked no questions.

The Prosecution was done. Only four and a half days later, and the Prosecution had presented their case. Jack said it was a smart thing for them to do, to come in with a lot of emotion and try for the slam dunk. It was very well conceived too, he said. The real brains were obviously sitting over there in the D.A.'s office. In general he felt good though, because he figured both sides had scored about an equal number of points. But we had the ball now, he said, and were perhaps only slightly behind. I didn't know if he was lying or not, if he was only trying to boost me up. With Jack you can't know, it's impossible, he never lets himself get negative and just dives into the next thing to do. But now it would be our turn with the ball, like he said.

I didn't know who the witnesses would be for our side. Jack only told me the first ones would be almost all character witnesses. Since it was a trial solely for sentencing, character witnesses were allowed, and he said he would parade half the damn town in front of that jury if he thought it would help.

He started with my basketball coach, and of course Coach couldn't say enough good things about me. Then Jack brought in five different teachers, one from middle school and four from the high school. And although they were in a real difficult situation and it really hurt, I could see that on their faces, they went on and on about how I was this real great kid to have in class, and about how intelligent and conscientious I'd always been.

Then, just before we broke for lunch, Mr. Babcock, the principal, came back in, but this time called as a witness for the Defense. The Prosecution was up in arms. They called for a recess. Jack just shrugged his shoulders and said, "They've had the list since yesterday, Your Honor, the same as you have." The judge told her to sit down again. Then, under questioning, Mr. Babcock said too what a great student I'd always been, a perfect role model for the school. And what he said was pretty impressive I guess, at least according to Danny, I mean coming from someone who'd gone through what he had. Jack thanked him when he left the

stand, told him it took a lot of courage. Jack had figured that the
Prosecution wouldn't dare cross, not since Mr. Babcock had been
one of their main witnesses. He was right. The prosecution had
no questions.

We broke for lunch. As usual, me and Jack and Danny had so
much to go over that we hardly had time to eat. At first we went
over what was said in the morning session, and then both Jack
and Danny changed. They became serious in a way I hadn't seen
until then. Jack told me that the testimony of the next few witnesses may prove difficult for me. Then he said he'd talked to my
mother, that she'd been the one to give the go-ahead, who'd
helped conceive the whole approach, and that she even provided
the information on which he would base many of his questions.
"But it may be difficult for you in there, Philip," he said. He put
his arm around my shoulder. "Just remember what our goal is.
Remember to keep your eye on the ball."

After the lunch break, the next witness we called was my biological father. I didn't expect it, but I wasn't surprised. Jack took
him back to when it all happened, when he first met my mother.
He said they met at a Vietnam veteran's place, a clinic like place.
She was a counselor there. They went out for a few months. When
asked if he was in love with her back then, my biological father
said he was, very much so. Then my mother got pregnant, he
said. And she pretty much freaked. That's the word he used too,
freaked. She didn't want the baby. He wanted more than anything to get married and have the baby. She refused. She wanted
to get an abortion. In those days, abortions weren't so easy to
come by. One day he went over to my mother's apartment, and
Mom was in bed looking real sick, real pale. A girlfriend was there
too, sitting by the bed. She was crying. My biological father didn't
know why. He thought it was odd. After, the girlfriend told
him that my mother had been in bed with a tube up in her self,

a rubber tube of some kind, trying to abort the baby. So he didn't want to, on top of his Vietnam experience this whole thing was destroying him, he said, but he finally ended up by giving her some money and she flew out to California. He thought it was long over, that she'd had the abortion, when one day he got a brief, sharp letter in the mail telling him he had a son. The letter had come from Indiana. There was no return address. He searched phone books, made hundreds of phone calls, even hired a private detective, but couldn't find a trace of her and the baby. Then, ten or so years later, out of the blue, he received a couple of letters, then a couple of phone calls, and one day there I was at the airport. He said he hadn't expected it to be, but it was by far the happiest, the most fulfilling day of his entire life.

The prosecution had no questions.

The next witness we called was my mother. From what Jack had told me at lunch, I expected it. She came in through a side door and walked to the front. She'd been crying, her eyes were all red, but she looked real pretty. Jack took her back to that time too, and she said what my biological father had said. Then she talked about after, about living with my stepfather, and then living the last ten years with Sidney without getting married. When asked why she never got married, for the sake of the child, she said she was afraid for her career, and that she was in a relationship where she basically didn't love the man to begin with. So why was she in it?, Jack said. Probably for purely security and financial reasons, my mother said. Then Jack asked her if she didn't realize the kind of psychological impact that could have on a child? She was a counselor, after all, didn't she realize how I could be negatively impacted by such a sterile, loveless relationship, and for ten years? My mother began to cry then. She said I'd always been the strong male presence in her life, that I'd seemed so much stronger than her, so much more mature. If any comforting was to be done, I was usually the one who had to provide it. She kept herself busy, as busy as she could, running from this, running from that, because she knew she could never be an adequate mother. Look at what she'd tried to do to me in the beginning, she said. How could she ever make up to me what she tried to do then? She really cried now. She could always feel my resentment, she said. But I didn't know what she meant. I always thought she like chose to have me by herself, alone, that's all, like she said. How could I resent her? When I was little, I never knew any of what happened back then.

Jack asked questions for a long time. It was real hard on my mother. I wanted him to stop, I didn't think it was necessary to dig so deep, but I tried to keep my eye on the ball. When he was done, Rachel King stood up. I don't think Jack expected it. But she stood, and walked out from behind her table. She took a few steps toward the stand. My mother still cried. Rachel King told her to take all the time she needed to calm herself down. She even brought her a fresh glass of water, passed her a tissue. My mother said thank you. When my mother was ready, she said, "I'm sorry, you can go ahead now."

"Oh that's quite all right," Rachel King said, "it's totally to be expected."

When she said that too there was something hard about her voice, I can't explain it, but something sarcastic. She folded her arms.

"Are you all set now?" she said.

My mother nodded.

"Good," Rachel King said. She looked at the floor, her arms still folded, and then looked back up. "You did say you were a professional, didn't you? A developmental counselor, working with children?"

"Yes."

"Well, among your friends, or among the parents of your clients, are there women who are divorced?"

The question surprised my mother, I think.

"Yes, of course," my mother said.

"Well, how many would you say?"

Jack stood up.

"Objection, Your Honor," he said. "Irrelevant."

"Overruled. If you recall, Mr. Shapiro, this has directly to do with your questioning on the family."

Rachel King looked up at the judge and nodded.

"Thank you, Your Honor," she said. She looked back at my mother. "Now, answer the question, please. How many of your friends, or parents of your clients, would you say are divorced?"

"I don't know. Half, perhaps?"

Rachel King nodded.

"All right," she said. "Let's say half. Now, all of that half, of course, have children, the children that see you."

"Of course," my mother said.

"And of those children, how many live with their mothers as opposed to their fathers? A majority, a minority?"

"A majority."

"Would you say a great majority?"

Jack stood up.

"Objection, Your Honor, badgering the witness."

"Overruled," Judge McLaughlin said. He looked down at Rachel King. "But please, let's get on with this, counselor. Get to the point."

Her eyes hadn't moved from my mother.

"So, would you say a vast majority then?"

"Yes, I suppose so."

"And would you agree, that for most of those children, I mean in real terms, in their day-to-day living, most of those children live without their fathers?"

"Well, there is joint custody," my mother said, "and . . . I don't know, other arrangements that can be made."

"Yes, fine, but if the father should happen to live more than a few miles away, joint custody is not feasible, wouldn't you agree?"

"Yes."

"And for these children in that situation then, they, in real terms, they in fact live fatherless for the vast majority of the time."

"Yes, I suppose so," my mother said, although I could see she didn't agree, only said it just to say it.

"Well then, of those children, of which there are millions and millions in this country as we speak, of all those children, how many that you know of go out and commit capital crimes such as murder?"

Jack shot up beside me, screaming. The judge gaveled, and even stood up behind the bench, gaveling and screaming at the top of his lungs.

"Strike that last remark! Strike that last remark!"

Rachel King did her best to look surprised. Judge McLaughlin was pissed, really pissed. He shoved the gavel towards her face.

"Counselor King," he said, "I want to see you over here! Now!"

He pointed to the opposite side of the bench from the witness stand. Jack began to walk over, but Judge McLaughlin waved him back.

"You just stay right over there, Mr. Shapiro," he said, still waving that gavel. "I'll take care of this."

Rachel King walked over, with almost this little smile on her face. The judge was furious. He was supposed to talk low, but everyone could hear him. A thousand dollars for that little monstrosity, he'd be writing her up for possible censure, and one more stupid goddamn sophomoric idiotic stunt like that in one of his courtrooms, and she'd be out on her ass for good. When Rachel King walked back to her table though, she still had that little smile on her face. Judge McLaughlin regained the bench, took a few deep breaths, and looked over at the jury.

"Now, members of the jury," he said, his voice very serious, "you are to completely disregard that last remark. Do you understand? Completely. It was totally irresponsible, and totally irrelevant. You are to disregard it completely."

Over at her table though, Rachel King still made that little smile.

The judge called a fifteen-minute recess, to calm things down. Jack shot right over to the Prosecution table and went right up into Rachel King's face, shouting stuff I couldn't make out. Danny and the bailiff ran over and had to pull him back. I'd never seen him so mad. I was surprised. He never loses his cool. Never. And some of the jury members were still walking out when he did it too. That's why I wonder if it wasn't on purpose. He was really mad, there's no doubt about that, but he's a guy who never loses his cool.

During the recess, Jack looked worried for a few seconds. He had a look in his eye that was new. Then he just seemed to shake it off. He said that, in general, he liked the way things were shaping up. Then he said he hoped that this last witness coming up, our last witness, would be his coo da grass, whatever that is. And before we knew it, the fifteen minutes were up. Judge McLaughlin was on his way back in.

When things settled down, Jack called Mr. James Gray to the stand, Missy's father. I was surprised. I think a lot of people were. The courtroom went even more quiet. Mr. Gray walked in through the side door. He's tall and thin. He works at the mill, still does, up in the office, and he's a really nice guy. He took the stand, and was so nervous that when his voice came out it was hardly above this little squeak. Judge McLaughlin had to ask him to speak up. Mr. Gray cleared his throat, and spoke louder. Throughout all the time he talked, he kept clearing his throat. Jack asked him how it came about that he was a witness for the Defense; "After all, your daughter, Melissa, she was one of those that died. Isn't that right?"

"Yes," Mr. Gray said.

"Then, how do you happen to be here?"

"I volunteered," he said.

"You got in touch with me, is that correct?"

"Yes."

"And would you please tell the court what you told me on the phone."

Mr. Gray cleared his throat again, moved in his chair. His long bony hands were stretched out in front of him, on the rail. They kept moving, nervous. He didn't know where to put them.

"I told you that I, uh, wanted to come and testify for Philip, uh, on Philip's behalf."

"And why was that, Mr.Gray?"

"Because I didn't want him to, uh . . . I don't know the correct way to say it."

"Just say it the way you said it to me on the phone."

"I didn't want him to be killed, uh, to be executed."

"Even though your daughter was one of those that died on the morning in question?"

"That's right."

Jack waited a few seconds. The courtroom was real quiet.

"Was this solely your idea," Jack said, "to come in here and testify on the Defendant's behalf?"

"No. Mine and my wife's," Mr. Gray said. "She, uh, she was the one who was going to come in and do it, but she's, uh, she's still not feeling too well."

Jack took a deep breath and bowed his head.

"Well, we can all surely understand that," he said. "Now, Mr. Gray, how long have you known Philip, the defendant?"

"Ever since he was just real little, two or so years old I think. My wife used to babysit him during the day back then, that's how he and Missy became so close."

"Missy. That's your daughter, Melissa. Right?"

"Right."

"Now, would you describe your relationship with the defendant as a close one?"

"Oh yes," Mr. Gray said. "Like I said, he was with us practically every day until he started school. And then my wife had him a lot after that too, if his mother was working."

"Well then, how would you describe your relationship, between the two of you?"

Mr. Gray was on the verge of tears. That was real hard to watch. That was probably the last thing I ever wanted to see in my life.

"I'd say a lot of the time he was just like my own son. At least it felt like that a lot of the time when he was young."

"What was his character like, his personality? Was he a likable child, a good child, well behaved?"

"Oh, I don't know so much about the well behaved part," Mr. Gray said, and he even kind of smiled, "he was a little boy after all. But he's a great kid, he really is, the very best. A person couldn't wish for a better son."

"And you would still say that, even today?"

"Oh yes," Mr. Gray said. "Oh yes." His voice was getting weak. His hands didn't know where to go. He looked out at Jack. "Look," he said, "I don't know what happened that day. I don't. I just don't know. This whole thing's such a tragedy, that's all, just such a terrible tragedy."

Mr. Gray bowed his head. He began to cry, not out loud, but real quiet. You could tell by the movement of his shoulders.

"No further questions, Your Honor," Jack said.

Rachel King stood. She waited until Mr. Gray had himself under control, then she stepped out from behind the table.

"Mr. Gray," she said, "I only have a few questions. And I'll be brief."

She gave Mr. Gray a few more seconds. She turned around to her table as if she had to check on something. She turned back towards the stand.

"Mr. Gray, how old was your daughter, Melissa, when she was murdered?"

"Seventeen," he said.

"How did she do in school? Was she a good student?"

"Oh yes," Mr. Gray said. "She did really well most of the time."

"An honor student, wasn't she?"

"Oh yes."

"She was elected to the National Honor Society, correct? And if I'm not mistaken, she was a National Merit Scholar?"

"Yes."

"And what were her plans after high school. I presume she was going to college."

"Oh yes. She'd already been accepted to Tufts. And then she was going on to Tufts Medical School. She had what they call an open acceptance. She could start any time she wanted to after high school."

"Tufts, you say?" Rachel King said, nodding her head. "That's a very difficult school to get into. Was she going in right out of high school, right after graduation?"

"No," Mr. Gray said.

"Oh, and why not?"

"Because she won this scholarship to study in Germany for one year, her freshman year in college. She didn't even tell us she was trying out for this scholarship. We didn't even know anything about it until she won."

"You were pleased?"

"Of course," Mr. Gray said. "We were worried too. I mean it's a big step to send your daughter off to a foreign country like that, especially if she's never left the house before, but of course we were pleased. We were really excited for her."

Rachel King waited, glancing at the floor.

"And what did Melissa plan to be, Mr. Gray, once she graduated from medical school?"

"A pediatrician. For some reason, ever since she was little, she always wanted to be a pediatrician."

Rachel King took a deep breath, and made this strange, very sad smile.

"My," she said, "it sounds like your daughter was a very idealistic, very intelligent young woman, Mr. Gray, with a full and interesting life ahead of her."

"She was," Mr. Gray said. "Yes."

"No further questions, Your Honor."

Beside me, Jack mumbled something and kicked the leg of the table. It was three in the afternoon on a Thursday. Mr. Gray had been the last witness. The testimony part of the trial had lasted only three and a half weeks. Everyone kind of stood around in the courtroom after, shocked. After all, O.J.'s had lasted a year and a half. And they knew Judge McLaughlin had a reputation for being fast, but not that fast. But next Monday the Prosecution would give their closing argument, and the day after that, on Tuesday, the Defense would give theirs. On the TV all that weekend, and in the newspapers, most of the reporters said that the way the jury would go was still up in the air, that much still depended on the strength of the closing arguments.

Right after court that day, Jack disappeared. Danny just said he'd be locking himself up in a room somewhere and not to worry, that, come next Monday, he'd be back in the courtroom with fire in his teeth.

When we walked into the courtroom on Monday, the Prosecution had the place plastered with those police photos again. There were even more this time. Someone had worked on them too, because the colors were really bright, the red really red. You could now see the tiniest detail of all the bodies. I was already dressed in my navy blue blazer, but Jack showed up with what he called this V-neck argyle vest, these kinds of diamonds on blue, and he made me wear it under the blazer. It looked stupid, like something out of one of those old fifties movies you see, with college students running around wearing saddle shoes, but that's what he wanted me to wear.

As we walked in, everyone was real tense, tight, right on the edge of their benches. No one said a word. The Prosecution was already at their table. Rachel King stood there, shuffling some papers. Then the jurors came in. They were tense too. Their eyes found a spot somewhere in front, then made sure they didn't move. The judge was announced. We all stood. When Judge McLaughlin was seated, he simply nodded to the Prosecution, to Rachel King, and said, "The Court's ready when you are, Counselor."

"Yes, Your Honor," she said, "If I could just have another few seconds, I'll be right with you."

She looked at some papers, fanned them out on the table in front of her. One of the lawyers beside her, a black lawyer, whispered to her, pointing out certain things on some of the pages. Then she straightened. She wore like this navy blue suit coat and a navy blue skirt. She pulled down a bit on the edges of the coat, then stepped around the table. She took a couple of deep breaths and turned towards the jury.

"Good day," she said, with a nice smile, "I trust you all had a good weekend. I know it hasn't been easy on you these past five weeks, but here we are near the end now, and we do all very much appreciate your dedication and your sense of duty."

She pulled on the edge of her suit coat again. Then she joined her hands, and took a step towards the jury.

"This is not an enviable task that I now have before me," she said. "I am a mother myself, a mother of three, and I will not conceal from you the fact that at times during this trial I too have been torn, as I'm sure you must have been, between my desire for justice and my equally strong desire for compassion. But there are times when our personal feelings, our personal emotion, must be put aside so we can clearly perceive the truth. And now, I'm afraid, is just such a time." She breathed again. She looked down real quick and then up. "Now," she said, "as you sit there I would like you to recall that you represent society. In a certain way, you are society. And yours is no small responsibility, for you must, in the name of all of us, seek to recognize the truth, to weigh that truth, then do your very best to make sure that justice is rendered. And justice can sometimes be severe." She hesitated here, taking another deep breath. "So, as you can see, in cases such as this, neither of us, neither you nor I, has an enviable task. But it is a task that must be done. Our perseverance, our very existence as an honorable and just society depends upon it." She pulled on her coat again. She took another step closer. "Responsibility. Let's remember that word. It is one of the basic building blocks, perhaps even the cornerstone, of any democratic society. I'm sure we can all agree that each mature member of such a society must assume full responsibility for his or her actions. Without the notion of individual responsibility, breakdown would occur, and inevitable chaos would ensue." Rachel King took a step closer to the stand. "Now, let me ask you to think about something," she said. She spoke very slowly, deliberately. "In the past forty years or so, what has happened to our notion of responsibility? Would you say that each of us is still held entirely responsible for our own actions? Or have we, on the contrary, created so many excuses for our behavior, so many reasons, that we can now act out whatever emotion we may feel inside, and act it out as outrageously, as violently as we like, knowing full well that the consequences will in no way fit the behavior? I'd like to have you think about that for a second." She turned away from the jury, walked over to the table, glanced at a paper, and then walked back. "Enabling. Now there's a bit of modern psycho-babble for you. Keep it in mind as I speak. Enabling. And what does that word mean, if not that we allow another person to shirk his responsibility, that we cover for him, make excuses for him? Yet, in essence, isn't this what we, as a society, have been doing for far too long a time now? Isn't this, in part, why we find ourselves in the moral straits we're in? Enabling. Please keep that word in mind. Isn't this what happens, too, when we seek to turn criminals into victims? In fact, where are the criminals nowadays? Have you ever stopped to ask yourselves that question? There are more killings than ever going on, more rapes, more violent crimes of every sort. We know that. We experience it. We live it. We have to lock our doors, carry around pepper mace, fear for our very lives; but where are the criminals? Have you ever wondered? The perpetrators have become either the poor misunderstood, or the poor abused, or, due to some past traumatic experience, the poor psychologically fragile, as if all those things somehow excuse their behavior. Even though they beat us, rape us, and kill us, they're not really criminals after all, we're told, they're basically very good human beings who need only to be understood, to be given a chance at rehabilitation." Rachel King's face changed. It tightened, became sarcastic. "Well, we've gone down that road, haven't we? For over two generations now, we've more than given it a chance to succeed. And I'll admit, when I went first went into law school, I was young and idealistic and ready to buy right into that philosophy myself." She was nodding her head. "Well, not only I, but the country as a whole bought into that philosophy, and I'll let you be the judge as to what kind of rewards we are reaping now. No one is responsible anymore. Just take a look at what has happened. No one is a criminal. No one suffers the real consequences of their actions. I mean, let's look closely at what has happened. We are becoming submerged in an epidemic of violence." She hesitated, looking briefly down at the floor. "And true to form, as we would expect in a case such as this, the lawyers for the Defense have been trying their best to paint the young man who murdered these people as a victim." She shook her head slowly. "A victim. Can you imagine that?" She turned fast then, real fast. She grabbed the pointer off the table. She walked over and just about slapped it against the first photo. "This is a victim!" she almost yelled, snapping it off the photo again. "Officer James Conrad, married, the father of two small girls, and murdered, an exploding bullet ripped through his gut!" She moved to the next photo. "And this is a victim! Officer Bill Hardy, recently married, the new father of a small baby boy, his thigh blown open, severing an artery and leaving him there writhing on the floor, bleeding to death!" Then she went to the next photo. "And another victim! Billy Jenkins, a freshman in high school, shot through the lungs while cowering against his locker, scared to death!" Then to the last photo. "And another still! Melissa Gray! What about Melissa Gray? Would you call her a victim?! A girl with a full and interesting life ahead of her! On her way to Tufts Medical School! Shot twice, once through the abdomen, once through the chest! I want you to take a good look at them! These are the victims! Yes! Not that neat-looking young man sitting over there in a blue blazer! Compare the difference between them if you will! Where is our common sense? Who are the real victims in this case?!" Rachel King hesitated, her face going hard. "And what excuse is there for such a crime?! Which excuse will we accept? Is being fatherless a valid excuse? Is being fatherless a valid excuse for committing whole-sale slaughter? Is being a good athlete, being a good student, are they all valid excuses? I don't care how many people take that stand telling us how admirable that young man over there is, this is still wholesale slaughter! And if we are ready to accept any excuse at all for this, well, then we, as a society, aren't we engaging in our own self-destruction?" She turned from the jury. She looked at all the photos, her arm outstretched. "Victims? We have victims! We have the victims, and we have the murderer!"

She walked over to the table and placed the pointer down real slow. She breathed deep again, and turned back towards the jury. "No," she said, her voice much softer now, "perhaps there are lesser crimes where we can weigh certain attenuating reasons, certain excuses; but for this crime you see before you? Is this one of them? Are we truly going to accept any kind of excuse for whole-sale slaughter? Don't we, as a society, don't we have to draw the line somewhere? For once, shouldn't the consequences fit the behavior, the punishment fit the crime?"

She breathed again real deep a few times, and folded her arms. Then she dropped them. She stepped up closer to the jury box. She laid a hand on the rail. "And let's talk a bit about this one crime in particular. Was it premeditated? We've heard testimony that the defendant was asked again and again by his best friend to get that gun out of the High School. And did the defendant make any attempt whatsoever to remove it? No, he didn't. He had five entire days we are told, during which he was in and out of the high school attending basketball practice, and never once did he even show the slightest desire to get it out of there. Premeditation. And his choice of ammunition. Let's have a look at that. The defendant fired not only exploding rounds, bullets that explode inside the body after piercing human flesh, but he also fired specially designed sonic rounds meant to enter the body, to make contact with bone, and then, through these high-pitch sonic vibrations, shatter that bone's entire length. You saw Principal Babcock. You heard about his wound. He was struck only in the shoulder, yet his arm, all the way from the elbow on down, has had to be amputated. Mere shards and splinters of bone, I saw the doctor's report, nothing left to be done. Premeditation. Why, in the name of God, would anyone have such bullets if not to purposely maim his fellow human beings? Does that fit with any kind of a spontaneous, spur-of-the-moment reaction that you've ever heard of, when the person pulling the trigger knows he is firing bullets specifically designed to kill and maim? And what about his standing there after the first three people have been shot, and killed, standing there in that hallway and aiming coldly, deliberately picking off the frightened rest, killing Billy Jenkins where he sat down there scared to death, cowering against his locker? Just a bad day was it, an abnormal reaction from a normally very good boy? In your minds, does that adequately cover it? Or can we perhaps conclude from all this that something in the psyche of this defendant, something very frightening and very dark, has escaped detection by even those closest to him? A victim? The person who did all this? Oh yes, he's truly the victim here, isn't he?"

She straightened and took her hand slowly off the rail. "Responsibility. Please remember that word. Without the notion of individual responsibility, a free and democratic society is doomed. And ponder as well this young man's good fortune in life. Think of it. How we would all love to have been born with his gifts. A star athlete, intelligent, good-looking, coming from an affluent home; he has surely been handed all the best this country has to offer, and yet, what has he chosen to do with it?" She looked up and down the jury then, looking at each of them. "Responsibility. How many lives have been devastated here? How many parents are childless, how many children are fatherless because of that young man over there? Responsibility. Where do excuses finally end and responsibility begin? When must the consequences finally fit the behavior?" She placed a hand back on the rail. "No, you must send a message here. You must. You are in a unique position to help us start turning all this around, to stop this madness, to warn people that they can no longer indulge in any behavior they choose without paying dearly for their actions. We must turn this around. The very existence of our society depends upon it. Justice must once again be served. These good people that you see behind me, their bodies ripped apart, their innocence massacred, they are demanding justice. Responsibility. It's the least we can demand of our citizens. The consequences must fit the behavior. The punishment must fit the crime." She hesitated. She rubbed a hand across her forehead. When she spoke again her voice was soft. She almost whispered. "I'm a mother. As a mother, I cherish life more than anything else. Do you really think that I could stand up here and ask for a capital sentence if I did not truly believe in what I say? Even though my insides cry out for me to be compassionate, I must realize that there are four human beings dead here, and seven others traumatized and maimed for life. I cannot serve two masters at once. I am sorry, I wish I could, but I cannot. The person who is responsible for this, who pleaded guilty to doing this, that person must assume the full weight of that responsibility. And so what does that mean exactly, the full weight of that responsibility? What shall we do? Shall we pat him on the wrist, and then fifteen or twenty years from now let him go free? Would that be justice for these people behind me? And who knows what further evil lurks in the soul of this man, I mean just take a look at what he is capable of. Could you forgive yourselves if, at some future date, such an atrocity were to be repeated?"

She laid both hands on the rail. "Responsibility," she said, still in that soft tone of voice. "Responsibility. Make the consequences fit the behavior. Make the punishment fit the crime. Send the message. Make it loud and clear. We are all depending on you."

Rachel King stepped away from the jurors box, rounded her table, and sat down. For a few seconds no on moved in the courtroom. Then Judge McLaughlin gaveled the session to an end, saying the defense would present its closing argument tomorrow at ten A.M. Everyone stood, but it was strange. No one talked like they usually did. They all just filed out real quiet. I didn't know what to think. Jack had often told me there would be times when I just had to block my mind, not let it jump to conclusions until all the facts were in. I guess this was one of those times. A couple of people were over there shaking Rachel King's hand. One was the district attorney, I recognized his face from the television. He was the one who always did the news conferences, but I'd never seen him in the courtroom before. When we were walking out Jack just tapped me on the shoulder and told me it was far from over. Her psychology was pat, he said, and if pat was what she wanted, why then pat was what she was gonna get. I didn't quite know what he meant. The way he said it surprised me too, he seemed pretty confident. Then he just disappeared again. Danny said he'd be locked back up in that room of his, rewriting his argument to respond to the Prosecution's.

Back in the police station, everyone was a lot more quiet than usual. They all looked at me in a different way. A couple of 'em tapped me on the shoulder and said, "How's it going, kid?" None of them ever called me kid before. None of them ever touched me before either. I blocked my mind like Jack said, but it wasn't easy. Up in my cell I forgot it all pretty much though, I usually do. It's like another world up there. There's just me and the bed, and the piece of sky out through my window. Sometimes I just sit and watch its light move in over there on the wall. And time passes. I never thought it would, but you always get to the next point somehow. I didn't know what Jack would say in the morning. I only knew it had to be good, real good. Those faces in the courtroom told me that.

For some reason, a part of me inside hadn't thought this was all that serious. That part of me still wants to tell me it's not, to tell me that something will happen to bring things back to normal, to make them be like before. And then there's another part of me, the biggest part, that just doesn't care. It's like it doesn't want to be bothered, doesn't want to get all excited about something it can't change. That's the part I don't want there, that I wish was more like Jack. He gets excited about everything. But it's your very own life we're talking about, that's what he yells at me all the time, so you'd think I'd at least be as excited about keeping it as he is.

Tuesday morning it was real nice out. It was the second of June. Out through my little window, the leaves on the trees were that fresh yellow-green like they get when they first come out. And I'd never realized how many birds there are that sing in the summer either. I only hear them dim through all of the concrete, but still, every morning they woke me up now about a half hour before sunrise. And a half hour before sunrise is early in June, real early. But I didn't mind. A lot of times, I'd even stand on my bed and wait for the sun to come up. Or not the sun really, because I can't see it, but I'd watch the sky go slow from gray to this white and into this sort of pink, before it jumps real fast into this deep deep blue. I'd never seen a sunrise before.

Tuesday morning, the courtroom was jammed again. I didn't see Jack until I walked in. He sat by himself down at the Defense table. There was nothing in front of him. He usually had his laptop open and a stack of papers, but he just sat there with his hands folded on the table. He stood when we arrived and let us move in by. He said good morning, and had this real open smile. I was surprised. He didn't seem nervous at all. Danny looked like he was about ready to shit in his pants though, no joke. He could hardly breathe. But Jack looked like he just got back from vacation. As usual, the Prosecution was already over there at their table.

Then the jurors came in, the court was called to order, and Judge McLaughlin walked in through the side door. He gave his greeting, arranged some papers, and then looked towards our table.

"We're ready when you are, Counselor."

"Thank you, Your Honor," Jack said. And then he just sat there. The whole courtroom was dead quiet. Everyone looked at him, and Jack just sat there. Then, I don't know how much time later, he pushed himself out from the table and stood up. He turned the table, and kind of like tapped it with his knuckle as he did. He walked real easy, not tense, not rigid at all like Rachel King had been.

"Good morning," he said to the members of the jury, with a nod of his head. "And we certainly do have a beautiful one going on outside this courtroom today, don't we? A beautiful, clear June day in New England. My, how fortunate you folks are to live up this way." He smiled, and nodded towards the Prosecution table. "And, as Counselor King has already so graciously done, let me second her expression of gratitude for your devotion and your sense of duty. Finding the truth, taking the time and the trouble necessary to find the truth, this is one of the most difficult and trying tasks that we can give ourselves. So again, both Ms. King and I do thank you deeply." Rachel King looked at one of her partners. She made this sarcastic little grin and kind of rolled her eyes. Jack looked down at his hands. He joined them together in front, looking real relaxed.

"Now yesterday," he said, "we heard a great deal about excuses, about excuses and responsibility. And you know, as strange as this may seem to you who have heard our more than occasional bickering, I do basically agree with most of what Ms. King had to say. What she so eloquently stated yesterday is a very basic truth, after all. We should all be responsible. We should never make excuses for our behavior." Jack took a deep and relaxed breath. "However, if I happen to be blind and must walk with a seeing-eye dog, can my state of being blind be called an excuse to have a dog? Or if I am truly sick for example, bedridden, and I can't work, can my sickness be labeled an excuse for taking the day off? In other words, can my physical state, the way I am, really be labeled an excuse?" Jack shook his head slowly. "I think not. I think we're mixing up our terms here. On the one hand there are excuses, and on the other hand there are realities. And being seventeen years old, at least the last time I checked, is a reality." Jack smiled. "And we were all seventeen once, weren't we? It's a long way back for some of us, I know, and believe me, do I ever know, but I'm sure we can still remember more or less what it was like. And if we have adolescents in the family, why then that reality is still all too fresh at times, I'm sure. Being an adolescent, or being the parent of an adolescent, is no smooth road. I know I don't have to tell any of you that. Emotion, irrationality, compulsiveness, despair, joy; it's all constantly flooding in and out, isn't it? The gates never shut. One day they think you're the greatest parent in the world, and the next you're the most mean, unforgiving jerk on the face of this earth." Some of the jury smiled. "Isn't that right? We've all been there, haven't we? It's the most volatile time in the development of a human being. And as far as being able to make sound decisions is concerned; would you say that this period in our lives is when we're best suited to make sound decisions, when we're popping around from emotion to emotion, from excitement to excitement, from idea to idea? I can speak only for myself, but I remember when I was seventeen I was madly in love. And I do mean madly. I was convinced that nothing could ever be deeper and stronger and more everlasting. I was ready to take on the world to prove it too, ardently, passionately, and of course the world at that time consisted mainly of my poor parents. Now, how they ever put up with that idiot kid of theirs without kicking his butt out the door still remains a mystery to me." Jack just kind of shook his head. Many of the jurors were smiling.

"Seventeen," he said. "Seventeen-year-olds making good decisions? Somehow, the two don't quite seem to go together, do they?" He straightened up. He waited a few seconds. "I have two adolescents of my own at home. And I look at it as part of my job as a parent to continually oversee their decisions. I give them a lot of leeway, want them to learn to decide for themselves, but I certainly jump in if I see that the results of their decision could be disastrous. And certain things I don't do. I don't allow them access to my bank account, for example. If I did, what do you suppose they would do? Do you suppose they would take my money and invest it in IRAs and in 401K pension plans, thereby procuring themselves a secure future?" Jack laughed a little. "I hardly think so. I rather believe they'd have the biggest stereo money can buy, the largest CD collection in the world, and more Mountain Dew than any mere mortal could drink in four lifetimes." The jury all smiled at that. Jack shook his head. "No," he said, "seventeen-year-olds, adolescents, they can, and do, make bad decisions. And this is a reality, folks, not an excuse." He turned around towards me. "And that boy over there," he said, pointing, "that boy is seventeen years old. Take a good look at him. You've seen him now for almost six weeks. Would you call him a mature man? He's seventeen years old, just seventeen by barely four months, and would you think him immune from all the predictable turmoil of a typical teenager? His body, his personality, everything is still in the process of forming itself. Nothing is stable. Bad decisions. Remember this: adolescents can, and do, make bad decisions. This is a reality, not an excuse."

Jack's face got a bit more serious then. His eyes darkened. He stepped closer towards the jury box.

"Now, let's take a closer look at the events leading up to that tragic morning. Plenty of bad decisions were made then, I'm afraid, too many bad decisions. The first was for Philip to take his friend Jason over to his uncle's house and show him the gun collection. The house was locked, Philip's uncle wanted no one in there when he wasn't around, but Jason had been wanting to see that gun collection for months, and so Philip, knowing where his uncle kept the key, took him over to show him. A bad decision? Yes. Completely out of the ballpark for a seventeen-year-old? Hardly. Philip was proudly showing something off, a bit of bravado, and how normal is that for a teenager?" Jack hesitated. "Then came the next bad decision, a worse decision. Jason suggested bringing the gun to school, and Philip, although at first resisting, eventually went along with him. A very unwise decision, especially in light of what is going on in the country today. But let's not forget that these two kids are from up here, hardly what can be called a metropolitan area. Their minds, I'm sure, tend to think differently. They still see the world a bit as it once was. They are not accustomed to constantly worrying about firearms, seeing firearms in school. It was a stupid decision on their part, no doubt about it, very stupid, but I'm sure quite innocent in its intent. They wanted to show off a bit at school, that's all. So they take the gun, and they put it in Philip's locker. Immediately, that evening, Jason realizes the bigger picture, realizes what is going on around the rest of the country, and he calls Philip to have it taken out. Philip, I'm sure, now realizes the stupidity of it all as well, but he lets it ride. Another very bad decision. He should've run right over there and taken it out. But no one else was aware at that point, and he knew he'd take it out eventually. And doesn't that sound like the typical thought process of a seventeen-year-old to you? Doesn't it? It'll get done. No problem. It'll get done. Whether it be the homework, or mowing the lawn, or cleaning up the room; no problem, it'll get done. And it hardly ever gets done, does it, at least not without a great deal of prodding. But is there any malice intended there? Can any reasonable person see any kind of evil premeditation? I don't think so. We've all done this same thing at some point in our lives, we've all run into this in our own children. Bad decisions. Bad decisions are a reality at this age, not an excuse."

Jack breathed real deep, looking away from the jury for a few seconds. Then he looked back.

"And so, we come to that terrible morning. The firearm is in the locker. Jason has heard that someone else knows about it. He also tells Philip that it means automatic suspension from high school if it's found. Forever. Philip hadn't been aware of this before. If he had, as responsible as this young man has proven himself to be, he wouldn't have brought that gun to school. But it's there now. And that morning they both hurry in to get it out. Philip opens the locker, and Jason goes back out to wait in the car, with the motor running. The plan is to scoot the gun out of the school as fast as they possibly can. But just when Philip is grabbing for his gym bag, down around the corner come the principal and the two police officers. At this point, you must understand that Philip has never been in any kind of trouble at school. None whatsoever. Never. In three and a half years, not so much as a single detention. He's an honor-roll student, a model student, those are the very words of his principal. He's also a star athlete. And so imagine this, if you will: You are seventeen years old, you've worked hard to get where you are, you've overcome a thousand emotional obstacles to get there, not the least being a pretty messed up home life, and in addition you're now getting scholarships literally thrown at you from major universities. But here, in this one moment, because of some foolish, unthinking prank, all of that is going to be swept away, erased. Imagine yourself in this situation. Imagine yourself being seventeen years old and in this situation. And now imagine those two police coming up towards you making threatening gestures. They have their hands on their guns. One of them shouts." Jack stopped. Just like that. His hands were in the air, forming a square. "And let's freeze everything right there. Let's freeze the frame right there at that one, single moment."

He was almost in a kind of crouch. His hands were still out in front, stopped in midair. No one in the courtroom budged, hardly moved even. Then he slowly dropped his hands. He straightened up.

"Now," he said, "as to what happened next, we all know. As to why, however, that has to be the one burning question for all of you. Why would a boy like this, do something like that? You must ask yourselves that over and over. And you've heard the testimony. You've heard how this boy is appreciated and loved by so many people in this town. And those people aren't fools. They weren't fooled by some evil, scheming demon. You saw them. They're regular people, intelligent people. They had nothing to gain by coming up here in their own home town and testifying for the very person who committed this act. As I've mentioned before, their gesture is unheard-of. Yet they risked their very reputations in this community to come up here and tell you what a good person that boy is." Jack was shaking his head in disbelief. "So you have to be asking yourselves, what is going on, what is happening here? Why would a basically good boy do something like this?"

Jack's face got that serious look again. He was stepping up to the plate. That's what he calls it whenever your time comes and you have to act. And that's what he had, that look he gets when he's stepping up to the plate.

"Realities," he said, stepping closer to the jury rail, "not excuses. And if we can agree that we're all here to discover the truth, and I'm sure we can, then we have an obligation to look at the one huge, overriding reality of any adolescent growing up in this country nowadays." He looked at each juror then, his eyes going real slow up and down the two rows. "Violence. And let me say it again. Violence. It's everywhere we look. You know that. Violence in the movies, violence on television, violence on computer screens. You can't get away from it. From all directions, our kids are being immersed in violence. When Philip, in the scared and confused state he must have been in, saw those two policemen coming towards him, shouting in a menacing manner and with their hands on their weapons, what do you suppose flashed through his mind? How many hundreds, no, how many thousands of similar scenes, each one erupting into explosions of incredible violence had been seared into his consciousness? And when I say that our children have been fed violence and bloodshed until they've become mesmerized by it, numbed, I'm not telling you anything you don't already know, am I? And if I add that a few of our so-called responsible citizens have made billions by pumping visions of violence into our children's minds, that wouldn't shock you either, would it? These are facts, after all, not excuses. Adolescents make great receptive mediums. If you want to make billions, why then they're naturals. Violence is intense. Violence is enormous. Violence is fast. Violence acts directly on the central nervous system. It's the smallest, least expensive pathway to achieving the greatest effect, and the greatest profit. You folks here are all very familiar with adolescents. When bombarded with such frenetic, such destructive energy, what adolescent couldn't help but be enthralled?" Jack stopped. He rubbed a hand over his mouth. He seemed to be thinking. "And let me share something with you," he then said, moving his hand away from his mouth. "Let me share this with you. I happen to have done a lot of pro bono work with drug addicts, with the homeless, with the less fortunate of our society. And do you know why crack cocaine is so addictive? Do you know why little kids, especially, become addicted so fast? When they try to describe the effect it has on their brains, that first explosion of the drug into their senses, they always describe it in violent terms. Intense, enormous, fast, blown away; these are the words they use. Interesting, isn't it? And the addiction is immediate, unrelenting, demanding to be reinforced with a stronger and stronger dose each time. That's very interesting, don't you think? And these are facts, not excuses. I'm talking about a purely physical response." Jack hesitated, maybe just giving the jury time to think. "And so you tell me," he said, nodding towards the jury. "You tell me. Do you think there may be a few so-called responsible citizens who know something we don't, who are keeping certain clinical evidence to themselves while they profit to no end from our children's vulnerability?"

Jack let the question stay out there a while. He folded his arms and looked at the floor.

"Realities," he then said. "Facts, not excuses. Our children are submerged in a sea of violent reaction. We see it everywhere. Not a day, not an hour goes by that their senses aren't somehow attacked, overloaded. The violent response has become the normal response."

He dropped his arms and looked up at the jury. His eyes opened wide and he had this strange little grin on his face.

"And do you know what? Do you know what the amazing aspect of all this is? None of it is real! That's right! It's all make believe! All of this violence exists out there on a screen somewhere, in a world of what is called 'virtual reality.' Harmless, the men making the millions have told us for years, absolutely harmless. And they would be right, I suppose, if we were dealing with people who have a clear view of themselves and of who they are, people who have a solid grasp of their own existence . . . but these are children we're talking about here. Children! Children upon whose backs we then heap all the other anxieties of our modern age, until we now see all too well what we've produced: kids whose natural response to their own frustration is violence. And they may well see the violence only on screens, it may well not really exist, but when it hits their nerve endings and shoots up into their brains, these kids experience a real response. A response is a response, after all. How are their bodies supposed to know the difference between a real, or a virtual, rush of adrenaline?!"

Jack stopped. He stepped back and breathed. For a long time he just stood there and simply breathed.

"So, on the one hand," he finally said, his voice much softer, "on the one hand, they experience the response, but on the other hand they don't experience the violence. They get the rush of adrenaline, but they still don't know what true violence is. They're cut off from the reality of it. There's no real bloodshed, there's no real suffering, nobody's really been killed." He was pointing to his chest. "But inside," he said, almost in a whisper now, "on the inside, each child is being conditioned to feel as if he lives in a world of real and imminent danger. Let's not forget that. And let's not forget, either, that they're interacting only with machines when they're racing through all of these feelings, these emotions. You know as well as I do that our kids now relate more to technology than they do to each other. The television, for example, it's an old and beaten horse, yes, but one that deserves to be beaten even some more . . . we can call that technology, can't we? Do you spend more time relating to your kids than the TV does? Do I? Hell no. I don't have that kind of time. Who has that kind of time anymore?" He stepped farther back. "And so in the middle of all this mess," he said, throwing his arms open wide, "in the middle of all this, we give these very same kids access to exile in the kingdom <<< 149

weapons such as AK-47 assault rifles, and we expect nothing to happen?! We dare to throw up our arms in amazement when atrocities occur?! I mean, c'mon! Are we really so naive? This is happening all across this country of ours! This is not some isolated event. Look in the newspaper! There are human tragedies such as this going on somewhere every day!" Jack had that look again, that real serious look. "Kids will always find a way of reaching out," he said, jabbing a finger through the air. "They will always find a way of expressing their frustration and trying to have themselves understood. They will always yearn to be understood. Anyone who knows anything about children knows this. 'No one understands me'; how often do we parents hear that refrain? And as sad and as tragic as this may sound, these kids are indeed reaching out, for they are communicating with us in the way they've been conditioned to communicate; through violent confrontation."

Jack's shoulders rose. He shook his head slowly again.

"So we've got the question wrong, haven't we? 'Why would such a boy do such a thing?' That's the wrong question. That's the cart before the horse again. The real question we should be asking ourselves is, 'Where were we when all this was going on?' That's the right question, the only honest question. After all, we are the adults in this situation, aren't we? This is our watch. Adolescents make bad decisions. We know that. Adolescents are vulnerable, easily influenced. We know that as well. So tell me, where have we been during all of this? And speaking of responsibility: What about ours? This is our watch. And this situation didn't develop overnight, it's been developing for decades. We've let it happen. And now we find ourselves in a real mess. Pandora's out of the box, and we don't know how to put her back in. The very fact that I'm here having to represent this boy proves it. But are we now going to start executing our children because of our own negligence?" Jack stopped. He stepped towards the jury box. He put a hand on the rail. He leaned forward. "Are we now going to execute our children for having swallowed what we so carelessly let be shoved down their throats? That would certainly be the easy response, wouldn't it? To answer violence with violence? Deflect the blame, feel secure for a while, and then execute the next child who reaches out to us in the only effective way he has learned to reach out, in the only way he thinks we will finally pay him any real, human attention?"

For the first time Jack looked tired, exhausted. He sighed. He shook his head, still leaning on the rail.

"No, violence is no solution and we know it. Violence is the problem. Executing a boy like Philip is not going to help solve anything. Deep inside, you must all know that."

He released from the rail. He turned and took a few steps away, as if he was finished. Then he stopped, and turned back.

"Oh, and by the way," he said, stepping up to the rail again and putting both hands firmly on it, "the Prosecution has it wrong. You don't represent society. That's not your job here. If this were Germany under Hitler, or the Soviet Union under Stalin, would you still consider it your duty to represent society? I sure hope not. No, your job is not to represent society, your job is to represent the truth. Societies come and go, but the truth never changes."

Jack leaned even more forward, with both hands still on the rail.

"Now, my client has pleaded guilty to this crime," he said; "therefore, he accepts full responsibility. And I stand before you making an old-fashioned plea for his life, to beg you for mercy. Mercy is the sister of truth. If you understand the truth of a situation, and weigh all the evidence in its proper context, mercy will almost always follow. There are a few exceptions to that rule, and I've seen men so hardened with evil that they do indeed deserve to be executed, but that boy behind me, and you've heard all the testimony to this effect, that boy over there is certainly not one of them. And by all means, yes, let's send a message. Let's tell the world that we refuse to slip back into the Dark Ages, that we will not start executing our children out of our own sense of frustration."

Jack released from the rail, standing upright.

"So I stand here before you now, begging for mercy. That boy over there is a good boy. And as Melissa Gray's father has said, and said so simply from deep within his suffering; 'This is all just such a tragedy, just such a terrible tragedy.' Please, we of the Defense beseech you, please find it in your hearts not to make it an even greater one."

Jack stepped away from the rail. He walked back towards the table. Danny pulled out his chair, and Jack just about fell into it. He looked exhausted. Everyone in the courtroom was dead quiet. Judge McLaughlin cleared his throat. Then he turned towards the jury. He told them the evidentiary portion of the trial was ended, that it was now time for their verdict, or, in this case, he said, their finding on the sentencing. Then he gave them their instructions. When he was finished, the jury rose before anyone else and left the courtroom. That was the first time they'd ever left before the judge did too. Then Judge McLaughlin left, and everyone just kind of hung around in the courtroom whispering. It was strange, like no one wanted to leave.

I wanted to though. I mean I was starved. They only give you one cold slice of toast and a dried-up egg for breakfast, and so by noon I was always starved. But for quite a few minutes Jack didn't move. He just sat there and looked exhausted. Finally, the bailiff came over, put the cuffs on me, and took me away to have lunch by myself. I hoped to eat it with Danny and Jack like I usually did, like I'd done almost every day for the past three or four months, eating Chinese or Thai or anything else I wanted, but Danny just nodded at me to go. He said he'd get in touch later on in the afternoon.

hat came then was the worst time, at least for Jack and Danny. They were nervous all the time, stiff as boards. They didn't know what to do. Sometimes we'd sit downstairs in our office for hours and they'd stare at the walls. They'd sigh over and over again, not saying anything. I hated it. I'd've rather been up here. Up here at least I can find things to think about. It didn't seem to bother me as much. I had to wait just like they did, but I'd waited all along anyway, and so I guess I was more used to it. On TV, half the commentators said that if the jury was out for a long time it was good for me, and the other half said it was bad for me, so I just tried not to think about it. I did ask Jack what he thought though, about the length of time the jury took and what it might mean for the decision, and he just told me not to believe any of the speculation, that each jury was unique and the length of time indicated nothing.

And the jury was out a long time. By Friday afternoon we still hadn't heard anything. That part at least was longer than O.J.'s. His jury was only out like about a day and a half. Jack went back to New York for the weekend. Danny stayed here in case the jury asked for ballots. They didn't. Jack came back on Monday, and there still was no word from the courthouse. Jack said there had to be a lot of wrangling going on, a lot of debate, with people not wanting to give in, one way or the other. He didn't come right out and say so, but the way he said it made you think it was good for our side.

Then, Tuesday morning, the jury asked for ballots. That just meant they were taking votes though, not that they were ready with a decision. But Jack and Danny called it "movement." They became even more nervous than before, if that was possible. They didn't even sit down. They'd lean on the walls, walk back and forth, and Danny used to be a heavy smoker, so he was sucking on this pencil all the time.

One more day went by. Then, Wednesday morning, we got word that the jury had reached a decision. Court would be in session at two o'clock that very afternoon.

We had lunch together in the office, a real quiet lunch. Then we all stood around until the bailiff came in to get me at quarter to two.

That afternoon, outside through the glass on the ramp going up to the courthouse, all the trees were this real rich green under a deep blue sky. I remember that. As usual, crowds of people filled the streets and started running towards the courthouse when they saw us. Jack and Danny walked ahead of me. It had been a week since I'd been in the courtroom. When the doors opened, it felt nice to be back inside. The dark brown shiny wood and the lights, it just brings you back to a different time and makes you feel real comfortable. And the place was jammed of course, and quiet, really quiet. The Prosecution's side was filled with the families of the victims. At the beginning, they used to stare at me when I came in, with these real hard cold stares, but after the first week or two they never looked at me at all. Today they didn't look either. We walked down and sat at our table. Then Judge McLaughlin came in, even before the jury did. He gaveled the session to order, then cleared his throat like he does. Even he seemed nervous, and he never seemed nervous.

"It appears the jury has reached its finding," he said. He nodded to the bailiff. "If you could bring in the jury, please, Officer Drew."

The bailiff walked over by the jury box, opened the side door, and the jury started to file in. And they looked awful. They looked tired. Their faces were all white, like ashes. Danny looked down at the table. Jack had his hand on my shoulder. The judge asked the jury if they'd reached their finding. The foreperson of the jury, a man, stood and said they had. He held a piece of paper in his hand. Judge McLaughlin then asked the court clerk to go over and get the piece of paper. She went over, took it from the foreperson, and then handed it to the judge. The judge read it, showed no reaction, none, even though everyone was trying hard to see one, and then he gave it back to the court clerk. She then handed it back to the foreperson. Everyone else in the jury had their heads down. I could feel Jack's hand squeeze my shoulder. The judge nodded to the bailiff.

"Will the defendant please rise and face the jury," the bailiff said.

We rose and faced the jury. Jack stood beside me, his hand still on my shoulder.

"You may now read your finding," Judge McLaughlin said, nodding towards the foreperson. "And please read it loudly and clearly."

The foreperson was real nervous. He was tall and skinny. He had one of those Adam's apples that stick out, that make a big bump and move up and down when the person talks. He opened the piece of paper.

"The Defendant having previously pleaded guilty to all the charges before him," he said, his voice so nervous that it shook, "we, the members of the jury, and in strict accordance with the laws of this state, do hereby sentence the Defendant, Philip Andrew Carmichael, to be administered a lethal injection until such time as he can be declared legally dead."

I don't know what I felt. Two of the women on the jury started to cry. Someone screamed no in back of me, real loud. Maybe it was my mother, but I don't know for sure. Jack's head was on my shoulder. Over on the other side, people cheered a little, but just a little, and then they stopped. I just stood there. I don't know what I felt. Jack said something about we'll appeal, don't worry Philip, we'll appeal. But I don't know what I felt.

They'll be changing my facility in two weeks. I don't want to leave here, but I guess the law says I have to be in a maximum security facility, in a special section designated for prisoners like me. I guess, too, that I'm the only one like me in the whole state though, so I'll be living in the section alone. I'm alone here, but it's my hometown and a lot of people come to visit. The maximum security facility is about a hundred miles away, down on the coast, so it won't be the same.

Jack got them to keep me here as long as he could. It's gotten so now I see people all the time. My mother comes in every day. Cheryl comes in three or four times a week. And then Reverend Mitchell pops in any time he wants. He just walks right up the back stairs. He's the only one they let do that. He's the only one I'd rather not see too, so I guess it figures he's the one I'd see the most. He's very upset, deep down I mean. He tries to hide it but it's always right there on the surface. He can't talk to me for five minutes without wanting to pray again. He doesn't say anything about my soul, not the exact word, but I know that's what he's worried about. And I don't like the feeling. It's strange to have someone beside you who sees beyond your body, who talks to something that's not even there. Before we pray, he always asks me if I've opened myself up yet, if I'm receiving God. And what can I say? I can't tell him the truth. I can't tell him that when we pray I hate it, that his words sound far away and just drop, drop like these drops of cold water hitting off metal. I can't tell him that. But that's the way his prayers sound to me, so I just close my eyes and try not to listen. I wish it wasn't like that though. I do. I mean, I'm in a perfect situation to like hear voices and get the big beam of light and stuff, like you read in the Bible. That would be great, and I keep waiting for that moment, for the voice and the light to stream in through my little window up there, but it hasn't happened, at least not yet.

I think a lot of things don't happen because I'm so young. For example, I don't seem as concerned or as sad as everyone else about the fact of, you know, about the fact I might die. Most of the time it doesn't even enter my mind. I know that has to be because of my age. As people grow older, death must become a bigger part of their life. It has to. You are getting closer to it. But maybe I don't care as much because I haven't had time for that to happen. I don't know, but people must form some kind of an idea as they move towards it. At least that sounds logical to me. I mean it's out there pressing closer and closer. But sometimes I almost think it's something in the blood. I do. People don't think about it maybe but it just starts settling in their blood, like making it thicker or something. I watch Grammy and Grampy, and when they move you can see their bodies aren't free any more. Something's settling in. I get aches and pains too, but my mind goes right through them in a second or two, forgets them, and then my body just follows along with no sweat. But their body can't, I don't think. I'm sure their mind tries to, like mine, but their body just can't follow along anymore. That's what I mean about the idea I guess, life forms it for you. You don't really have to think about it, but as you move towards death, life has a way of making you realize it's there. And that's what I don't have. Nothing tells me it's there. But it is. Jack says he'll appeal and appeal, but the newspapers say that a jury's sentence is seldom overturned, if ever. In this kind of case it's never even happened before. The courts won't touch it, because of what they call the integrity of the system. So nothing tells me it's there, but it is. No one will tell me when either. Jack doesn't want to talk about it because he don't really believe it yet. But in the papers and on TV they say no more than a year. A year. Most of the time, that sounds like a long way off to me.

I don't know why I did what I did. Sometimes I believe what Jack said, at the trial. It sounded good. But that was Jack talking, and most of the time I think it's just nice-sounding stuff he made up to try and get me off the hook. And I don't feel all that awful about it. That's what's strange. I don't. I mean I feel awful that it happened, but I'm not tortured by their faces night and day. I think I'm supposed to be, though. I do see Missy's face. But I see it that night at the hotel, when she came out of the bathroom. She was just so mad, it was so deep. At the time, I didn't know why. I knew how she could be upset, but I didn't know who she could be so mad at. Sometimes I wonder if I was mad that morning, but I've got no one to be mad at either.

I see a psychiatrist three times a week now. It was mandated by the court. And all we do is talk, no more stupid fucking tests. He's a nice guy, but he talks about being mad too. He talks about what he calls my seeming indifference. Like Danny, he says it could have been misinterpreted by the jurors. And lately, he always asks me if the distance, if the seeming indifference in the way I am, in the way I speak, if I think it's just an attempt to conceal what he calls a measured rage. But how should I know? I don't think so. I've never felt indifferent, I never have. And the way I speak is the way I've always spoken. I mean no one ever bothered to read all this shit into how I am before.

After the trial, I saw a couple of the jurors interviewed on TV. They said the reason for voting like they did was the kind of bullets in the gun. They seemed real sincere, and they said they were all ready to be lenient, wanted to be lenient, but they couldn't get past the idea of having sonic bullets and exploding bullets in the gun. One of them also said that Jack's psychology was just too pat, whatever that means.

Since the trial too, other things have changed around here. I get to go to this computer room down in the basement. I can go on the Net, and they've even got Doom II installed, but it's just more of the same old thing. I put it on chainsaw and then start whacking my way through a whole bunch of people, but it's really pretty boring. I don't know how I ever liked it so much. I get to play basketball more too. I can go outside just about any time I want now if the other inmates aren't out there. That's what I'm going to miss the most when I have to leave, that and my cell, of course.

I really like my cell now. That sounds stupid, I know, but I do. I can't believe I ever thought it would be boring up here. Sometimes on rainy days it is, because I can't see the square of light up on the wall, but on those days I just go out and play more basketball. When the sun's out though, I can just sit here on my bed for hours and watch its light move real slow across the wall. I don't know what I think of, but I can see like the particles of dust rising and falling along that stream, almost dancing in a wind when there is no wind, at least no wind that I can feel, even though it must be there or they wouldn't be dancing, and that's pretty cool. I don't know why I never saw it before. And the blue of the sky outside, I mean the sun sets now just over the river, and I love to stand here up on my bed and watch it go down so red, and feel it so warm on my face, with the river and the sky so blue all around it. Maybe that's why I don't care so much. I mean I'd probably care a lot more if I thought I wasn't a part of all that. Even if my mind tries to tell me I'm not a lot of the time, that I'm somehow different, I know that I am. When I look out sometimes, I'm the sun and I'm the river and I'm the sky, it's all in me, it's all outside of me, moving all the time. I never felt that before. I'm just a guy who happens to be like caught up in the ride, drifting up and down in my own little dance I guess, even though I can't feel the wind, and any way you look at it, that's really pretty cool.

about writing this book

The pivotal event in this work is the result of pure histor-ical coincidence. If not this, it would have been another. The "real stuff" always remains the same. And besides, any work that seeks to be topical in nature will also be topical in depth. The eyes of an adolescent, who lives a reality, absorbs and becomes its reflection. But this work is not an intellectual exercise. The farthest thing from it, or so I hope. The simple, direct, sensorial experience of a seventeen-year-old as he lives. Or feels. Or the void thereof. Which brings me to Camus, and *L'Etranger*. I read it years ago, the indifference, the consciousness running head first into the absurd and freezing, having to neutralize itself just to continue. That was in 1939. Well, we've all continued. And here we are. A few years ago, way before all that has happened since, I wondered what a young mind of today, perhaps one of my own students, would . . . and talk about your withdrawal. Camus saw nothing really, not compared to what we see every day. He was still firmly in the Industrial Age, after all. That even sounds quaint now, not to mention so terribly slow. And this is one consciousness, one style, one book. Please, do not extrapolate.

This work had a strange journey to get to this point (there are four others, all published, or soon to be, in France). I wrote it first in French. The two versions are as different as the two languages. The classical, poetic, clinically cold beauty that French can attain,

thanks to the Académie, English simply does not have. Spontaneous, ever evolving, adapting to the moment; that's our language.
And though enthusiastically received in France, and Quebec (even
to the tune of being in pre-production for an English-language
film), here in the United States, until now, only rejection. It reads
fast, however, and draws you in and all that good stuff, so why?
Forever the good Puritan, I tried my damnedest to blame myself,
the deficiencies of the work. France kept telling me no, that the
mirror held was not what America wanted to see. Too real, too
close. And the economy is expanding, after all. You people over
there do have your priorities. One headline in a major French
publication: "The book that scares America!" I, of course, thought
it was hype. Now, I don't know. Maybe they have something there.
Perhaps the problem is indeed the reflection in the mirror. But I'll
stop right here. We Puritans have to be careful while breathing
the rarefied air of self-confidence; it props us up an inch only to
drive us down a good foot. And there is no message in this work.
None. Or rather, the style is the message. The reader can feel free
to draw any conclusion he or she wants, resting assured that the
one they accept will be as shot full as holes as the ones they reject.

And finally, on to New England. I wish I could say I was from
New England, but I can't. I'm from Maine, 70 miles above Au-
gusta. And I'm not being flip here. This is the way I feel, we feel,
have always felt. Cape Cod, Kennebunkport, North Conway;
they're all creeping inexorably this way, bringing their neat and
sterile dream of what once was. Fortunately, just up the road, are
Quebec and New Brunswick, a natural brake to any realistic capi-
talists, be they liberal or conservative, hoping to redream the past
while making a fistful of dollars. I'm from here, grew up here.
Please don't ask any questions about how I feel about this place.
That a person should spend his life obsessing, seeking to find and
express the truth he thinks buried somewhere in this soil; that

should amply define the relationship. The Puritan framework. Up here, we're born to repress emotion. No emotion is worth a damn if it's not been repressed at least half a lifetime. Add to this the massive repression of authentic, real human emotion that technology demands, . . . and I guess that's as good a starting point as any for meeting the young man within.

And, outside at the moment, snow falling, a most marvelous thing, just watching it float down. In a few minutes, skiing in all that, the clean air, the fresh snow, the absolute purity . . . so the underlying reality is always optimistic, and, thank God, indestructible.

They don't want more "Mountain Dew" if they're poor, or more weekends at Stowe if they're affluent. Affection. Caring. Attention. *Wachet auf, Rußtuns die Stimme!*